I AM LYDIA

I AM LYDIA

J RYAN

The Book Guild Ltd

First published in Great Britain in 2023 by
The Book Guild Ltd
Unit E2 Airfield Business Park,
Harrison Road, Market Harborough,
Leicestershire. LE16 7UL
Tel: 0116 2792299
www.bookguild.co.uk
Email: info@bookguild.co.uk
Twitter: @bookguild

Copyright © 2023 By J Ryan

The right of J Ryan to be identified as the author of this
work has been asserted by them in accordance with the
Copyright, Design and Patents Act 1988.

All rights reserved. No part of this publication may be
reproduced, transmitted, or stored in a retrieval system, in any form or by any means,
without permission in writing from the publisher, nor be otherwise circulated in
any form of binding or cover other than that in which it is published and without
a similar condition being imposed on the subsequent purchaser.

This work is entirely fictitious and bears no resemblance to any persons living or dead.

Typeset in 11pt Minion Pro

Printed and bound by CPI Group (UK) Ltd, Croydon, CR0 4YY

ISBN 978 1915603 807

British Library Cataloguing in Publication Data.
A catalogue record for this book is available from the British Library.

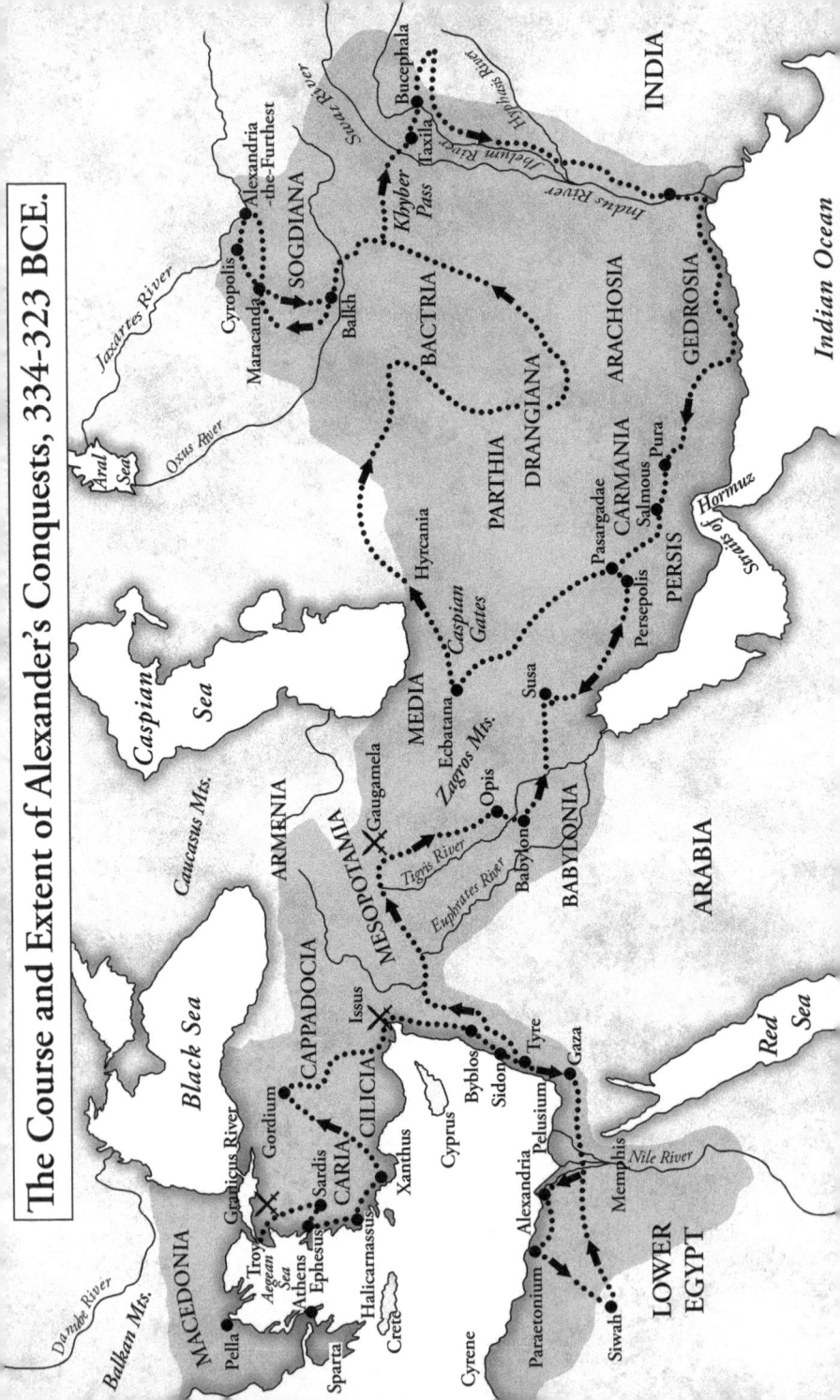

ONE

FASTER, HIGHER, STRONGER

I've never known an Olympic crowd to be so quiet. As I walk Pegasus down the line, shaking hands with each of my teammates, you could hear a feather fall. Xanthippe's dark eyes flash as she grasps my hand. Philesia's face is solemn and I tell her to cheer up, we're going to win. Then Penelope, totally in control of her young horse at his first Games. But this race is a first for everyone in it. Never before at the Olympics has there been a mounted archer relay. And never ever before have females competed against males.

Artemisia is grinning broadly; she can't wait to give our rivals a thrashing. So is her best mate, Callista; these two are invincible together. Now, as I take my place, I can feel Pegasus trembling with eagerness to run our rivals off their feet. This is his first Games too; I rode his sire at my first Olympics and he won me a gold. Peg knows that his father will be a hard act to follow; but when we raced the two of them a week ago, they were neck and neck. We're going last of the team, because if there's some catching up to do, Peg will do it best. Today, my black Arabian will dig deep for the power and the glory.

In the front row of the spectators, I can see my mother and father sitting motionless, their eyes only on me. Next to my father is Uncle Leon and his beautiful wife, Danae. And next to them, because they didn't get into the relay final, are their twin sons. I'm secretly glad that I'm not competing against the two boys whom I've grown up with so closely, they could be my brothers. I know that Damon wouldn't mind me beating him, but Lysander would hate it.

Now we're under starter's orders, the only female team to get into the final. Competing against a field of highly trained, seasoned cavalrymen. But the way I see it, we girls have the advantage. As my father puts it, 'A significantly better power-to-weight ratio.'

We're off, and Xanthippe has a superb start on her grey-dappled Thessalian, Heracles. She's ahead of the field as she disappears round the first curve, the red baton gripped firmly in her right hand. Halfway round is a jump with a ditch on the other side of it; when we walked the course, it was clear that you'd have to do a leap with some real height in it to stretch over that ditch. We let all the horses take a good look at it.

Xanthippe has held onto her lead as she thunders up to us and passes the baton into Philesia's waiting hand, stopping just short of the line. Everyone has to get off from a standing start or they're disqualified. Philesia's dark bay stallion, Marathon, goes straight into the leaping gallop which we've been practising for months. The other teams are cheering their mates on, but we save our breath, riding using our knees to lift our weight off our horses' backs, to help them use their hindquarters to the maximum. That was a tip of my mother's, who is almost impossible to beat, on a horse, in a chariot, or on her own two feet.

Our lead has decreased slightly as Philesia passes the baton to Penelope and I wonder if she had some difficulty at the jump. She looks at me. 'Got barged in mid-air.'

'Do you want me to mount a challenge if they win?'

She shakes her head. 'The man who barged us is in the ditch. They won't win.'

Penelope gallops up and thrusts the baton into Artemisia's grasp; in a thunder of hooves, she's away. But our lead is now very narrow. Penelope grimaces. 'Dirty tricks at the jump.' She looks at Philesia, who nods.

Callista's jaw is set grimly. 'So they'll doubtless be trying the same with Misi.' She strokes the neck of her sturdy golden chestnut, Ajax. 'We'll get them back for that!'

When Artemisia gallops in to pass the baton to Callista, we're now two lengths behind the leading team. She mutters to me furiously, 'They're all ganging up together at the jump!'

I say, 'I think your best mate is on the case.'

Only one horse and rider get started before Callista and her gallant Ajax arrive. Thrusting the baton at me she hisses, 'Got him!'

Pegasus takes a huge leap forward. The leading rider is now six lengths ahead. My aim is to get in front of him well before we reach the jump, so that he'll be nowhere near us when we take off. I whisper to my flying horse, 'Let's go!'

Digging deep as only the son of Arion the Arabian could do, Peg puts on a spurt that nearly shunts me off backwards. Suddenly, we're closing on the leader at a speed we've never hit before. Peg's black mane whips in my face as we draw level, and I don't even look as we shoot past, like a spear hurled by Achilles. We're two lengths in front, as the jump looms ahead; and I can see the churned ground where all the dirty work took place.

I let Peg choose where he will jump. We've all practised this too, many times. Your horse knows best how to take an obstacle, unless there is something he can't see; and Peg is well aware of the ditch on the other side. He takes the smoother path, on the outside, to get a secure footing, lifts off high and wide, and lands without a beat. Now he knows and I know that we don't have to flog ourselves to cross the finishing line ahead of the pack.

But there is one more challenge waiting for the final rider in every mounted archer relay team. Taking the baton in my teeth and letting go of the reins, I charge my bow and look ahead at the mark. If another rider hits the bullseye instead of me, the race will not be an outright win for us. A quick glance behind, and I can see the pack is gaining on the horse we overtook, and gaining on us. But the mark is now nearly within range. Closer. I let fly my arrow, and it whacks straight into the centre.

I am more startled than Peg by the roar that goes up from the spectators, as we canter across the finish line;

thousands are standing and cheering, flowers raining down. Lining up with my teammates for the gold, cool and calm, as Spartans always are, I glimpse a face in the crowd. He is not cheering, and he is looking directly at me.

*

I was twelve years old when I did my first Olympics. You might think that was quite young, but in Sparta you're trained up to be super-fit from your early years. Girls are trained just as hard as boys, side by side, and usually naked as well; so there's not much that I don't know about the boys in my life. My father says that there is no other Greek state like Sparta. From age seven, I was schooled in wrestling, discus-throwing, javelin-throwing, running, and swimming. From my mother and my aunt Danae, I learned horse-riding, bowmanship, and charioteering. While Uncle Leon taught me javelin-throwing and sword-fighting on horseback, and hand-to-hand combat on foot – the close-quarters fighting at which Spartans excel. And through my father and Uncle Leon, I learned to read and write, study philosophy, and enjoy Homer and Xenophon.

My father told me how he and Uncle Leon served under Xenophon to defeat a third Persian invasion of all Greece. He said that Xenophon's exile to Sparta had been ended after the victory, and he had been invited to return to his native Athens by his great friend Philemon.

And Philemon of Athens is the link to how I was given my name. My father told me when I was seven. He took me out riding, he on Arion and me on Pegasus: father and daughter on father and son. He told me about how he was sent as a spy to Athens by Uncle Leon, who was head of the Krypteia, Sparta's secret service, at the time. He was bought as a slave by a very kind Athenian nobleman called Philemon, and appointed tutor to his thirteen-year-old daughter, Lydia. My father told me how she could sing exquisitely and compose beautiful songs, and had extraordinarily good judgement. Then his voice trembled, as he recounted how she died, after having a stillborn baby, having married when she was far younger than we Spartan females are when we take a husband.

When my father told me this, huge tears rolled down my face, and Peg stopped walking when he felt my grief. My father got off his horse and took me off Peg's back into his arms. I was not a child who cried very much – except, my mother says, when I was a baby and was always hungry. Somehow, I felt that I had to do something with this sadness; that the name I had inherited should push me to be the very best that I could be.

I had always known that I was found on Mount Taygetos, and I knew that both my parents had come from the mountain too. This made me feel even closer to them than many children feel with their natural parents, and I know they feel that way about me. So when I asked my father if he would train me to be an armourer, like he had been before he became one of Sparta's two kings, he took me straight to the forge where he had learned his trade.

It was unbelievably hard work, and incredibly hot; it made me strong, and I loved it. As though through this fire, I could forge a future for myself that would commemorate my namesake and her beautiful singing. My father has a lovely voice. Uncle Leon told me that my father's voice saved his life once, singing Lydia's flying horse song. Father often sings that song. Every time I hear it, I remember who I am, and what I have to do.

After two years, I had become a skilled armourer and very strong. I made a suit of armour for myself and each of my teammates; we had decided that we wanted to be soldiers in the army. Not just any soldiers, but ones that Sparta very much needed. There were many excellent archers in the Spartan army, but very few who could deliver a really fast shock-and-awe charge on horseback. We called ourselves the Myrmidons, in tribute to Achilles' formidable troops. The only difference was that we were all females.

And the big difference between the Spartan army and those of other countries is that ours is the only one in the world where the only break in training for war is war itself. For Spartans, bravery is the ultimate virtue. Suicidal recklessness, misbehaviour, and rage are all prohibited in the Spartan army, as they endanger the other troops. Recklessness can also lead to dishonour; so can dropping the shield, failing to complete training, and deserting in battle. Dishonoured Spartans are labelled as outcasts and have to wear different clothing for public humiliation.

Spartans who fight, while still wishing to live, are regarded as more valorous than those who don't care if they die. A Spartan warrior must not fight with raging anger but with calm determination. Spartans must walk without any noise and speak only with few words, according to the laconic way of life. In battles, the Spartans tell stories of valour to inspire the troops; before a major confrontation, they sing soft songs to calm the nerves.

You start to understand these values from a very young age, because Sparta is the only state to provide a public education system, the agoge, for boys and girls. Here, both the body and the mind are trained. Spartans are not only literate but admired for our intellectual culture and poetry. The great philosopher Socrates, Xenophon's teacher, said the 'most ancient and fertile homes of philosophy among the Greeks are Crete and Sparta, where are found more sophists than anywhere on earth'.

Self-discipline, not mindless obedience, is the goal of Spartan education. My country places the values of liberty and equality at the centre of our ethical system. Just as, in the army, no soldier is considered superior to another. These values apply to every full Spartan citizen, immigrant, merchant, and even to the helots, but not to the dishonoured. Helots are unique among the enslaved, in that, unlike traditional slaves, they are allowed to gain and keep wealth. So, they can keep half of their agricultural produce and can accumulate wealth by selling it. There have been occasions when a helot with enough money could purchase their freedom from the state. And now that my father and Uncle Leon are recruiting more and more helots into the army, they are being paid and given land.

So you can see why, having gone through the rigorous Spartan education system, we girls felt that the logical next step for us should be the same as for the boys. My mother and Aunt Danae were in favour of us being in the army; at least until we reached twenty, when females are allowed to marry in Sparta. Even then, once our child-bearing days are over, I don't see why we shouldn't return to the military. Men are expected to keep themselves fit and remain in active service until they're sixty. Why not women?

But before we could get ourselves trialled for the army, there was an issue that I needed to tackle. I felt that we could shoot deadlier arrows if I could re-design the arrowhead. I sat and looked at it in the forge with my father. Made of iron, it had a two-lobed design with a shaft up the middle where it was attached to the stem. There was a nick in one of the ears, which was designed to cause more blood-letting if it was pulled from a wound. I said to my father, 'Why should we not have a nick in both of the ears? So that, whichever way up it enters our enemy's body, it will damage him further to try and remove it?'

My father is an inventor in every sense; he designed the renowned Achilles chariot that helped to win the last war against the Persians. And Uncle Leon says my father is one of the two most creative military strategists he's ever met (the other one is Xenophon). So I could see that my question had fired up my father's interest. Picking up the arrow, he weighted it and watched it balance in his hand.

Then, I said, 'And suppose we add a third lobe with a nick in it, Father? That would make the arrowhead stronger and even more penetrating.'

He replied, still balancing the arrow, 'Not only that, but probably more stable in flight as well. I think we need to test your theories, Liddy. Shall we start tonight?'

So that very night, we forged a number of iron arrowheads that had three lobes, each with a deadly nick in it. The next day, my chief Myrmidons assembled to try them out, with my father and mother and Uncle Leon looking on. Xanthippe exclaimed at the speed and accuracy of the new contender. When Callista and Misi went over to the dummies, it was impossible to remove an arrow without ripping the dummy to pieces.

My father looked at me with proud eyes and told me that I had made a big contribution to the Spartan army. He had my new arrows put into volume production immediately in the forges. And there would come a time when we Myrmidons were all very grateful that these iron birds with their deadly beaks were felling our enemies in the dust.

*

I know that Uncle Leon's feelings on the Myrmidons joining the army were mixed, but he agreed with my father that we should be allowed to take part in manoeuvres for an experimental period. My father and uncle can decide these things because they're Sparta's kings, who lead the military in battle, while the five ephors, who are elected annually, run just about everything else, including the elite youth secret service, the Krypteia. My father and Uncle Leon spend much of their time with the army and very often sleep in the barracks. Spartan kings don't always have this close relationship with the men they take to war; as a result, when the men learned that King Lycon's daughter would be leading their new all-female mounted archer squadron, the reaction was very positive. What helped was the approval that the new arrows had already won with the troops.

FASTER, HIGHER, STRONGER

The first step was for us to show how useful we could be. So two weeks later, Uncle Leon led us and a cavalry division to the assault course in the foothills of Mount Taygetos, where my father had supervised the construction of several lines of dummies stuffed with straw, roughly three hundred yards from the final jump. I had my five team leaders with me for this first trial – the same who would fly the course so brilliantly a few years later at the Olympics: Xanthippe, Philesia, Penelope, Artemisia (Misi) and Callista. The rest of the squadron – we were fifty strong – came along to watch and learn.

And now, I have to say that my native cunning had ensured that we would put on a good show. Guessing that this would be the setting for our trial, I had been practising with my team for the previous ten days, every day, for five hours at a time. As a result, each team member was skilled at breakneck downhill gallops, over seriously challenging obstacles. We had been doing shooting practice too – firing volleys of arrows at a man's chest height at the trees that populated the end of the downhill run. And, of course, collecting every single arrow carefully afterwards. If the army was using the course for practice, then we left ours until nightfall; that was far harder, so it made the daytime practice seem easier.

You're probably thinking that Uncle Leon would double-guess my plans. And you'd be right – after all, he was the leader of the Krypteia for years, and – my father can confirm – scarily good at getting into people's heads. But, as Xanthippe said, that would simply prove to him that we were every inch capable of supporting his soldiers. And when, on our last night of practice, we saw him waiting for us on Arion, the approving look on his face told me that Xanthippe was correct.

The following morning, as we assembled into battle formation with the cavalry at the top of the slope, Uncle Leon explained to the troops what this manoeuvre was about. Essentially, it was about speed. The Myrmidons would advance on the enemy at full gallop, firing volleys of arrows with the aim of downing the maximum number of enemy troops possible, in order to break up their line. This would make the subsequent cavalry charge all the more effective. Our speed – as well as Spartan armour – would make us almost impossible targets. Our horses, too, were well-armoured. And I figured we would look quite daunting, with our long hair flying beneath our helmets. Spartan men have a particular thing for long hair. Not only is it an ancient symbol of freedom, but Lycurgus, our legendary law-giver, is said to have claimed that long hair could make a beautiful man even more beautiful and an ugly one even more terrible. Many Spartan soldiers wear their hair long and comb it as part of their preparation for battle. So to the enemy we will look like men, except that we'll be riding faster than they ever will.

Uncle Leon finishes his explanation and gives me the nod. I raise my hand as the signal and we're off, our horses launching themselves at that obstacle-strewn slope on nimble hooves. I glance at my team, galloping pell-mell downhill in a perfectly even line, and my heart thuds with pride and excitement.

Behind us, I can hear Uncle Leon calling commands to the cavalry. I've positioned myself so that it's Peg and I who will tackle the ruin, because we have a plan to avoid it slowing us down. We're going over, not through it. In a move we've practised many times, he clears it in one enormous bound, landing perfectly balanced. Out of the corner of my eye, I can see Xanthippe on Heracles, taking a spectacular leap over the sheep pen.

Seconds later, we've jumped the final ditch, and we let go our reins to load our bows and start shooting as the dummies come into range. Our whistling arrows down the lot of them, and we thunder on to the end of the course. Uncle Leon's brief to the men was that the cavalry would take out with their spears any dummies that we didn't hit. I exchange a furtive grin with Xanthippe; we've left them nothing to do.

My father is waiting for us on Circe, the chestnut Arabian mare he plundered from the Persian army. He doesn't say anything as we form a well-ordered line, but his amber eyes are very bright. The cavalry, led by Uncle Leon on Arion, slows to a walk and lines up in formation opposite us. Like all of us except my father, he's in full armour, his eyes in darkness beneath the cockaded helmet, so I can't guess at what his thoughts might be. But I'm very proud of my Myrmidons, as they sit in silence on horses who stand perfectly still, without even a tail swish. Just as Xenophon's white charger used to do, my father tells me.

Then Uncle Leon removes his helmet, and the flaxen hair falls to his shoulders. His blue eyes are smiling even though his face is stern. He says, in his quiet voice, 'It would seem, Myrmidons, that the Spartan army has a new secret weapon.' And behind him, swords flash, as the cavalrymen raise them to the skies.

I AM LYDIA

*

My team leaders got straight to work after that, each training up their ten-strong cohorts to the same standards that we had achieved that day. In the meantime, I sat down with my father and Uncle Leon to discuss other practice scenarios. One, that I had read about in Xenophon's work, involved a river crossing, where the enemy had the advantage of steep banks and higher ground on their side. Another, where the enemy line outflanked us to either side due to superior numbers (something we Spartans are well used to); I explained how our mounted archers could deal with that. We also discussed pre-emptive strikes – a tactic that my father had introduced with devastating effect in the last Persian invasion.

In the run-up to the next Olympic Games, we honed our battle skills and our strength to a peak of perfection. My father and Uncle Leon were very proud of me. And Damon, who was by then an accomplished cavalry rider, saluted the contribution made by the Myrmidons. The only person who did not seem wholeheartedly in favour was Lysander, by now himself a polished cavalryman. Almost perversely, he never seemed to take the same viewpoint as his twin. My father said not to worry; teenagers can be famously contrary (I should know!). Which is why being in the army helps to keep them in check. But I felt uneasy about Lysander. There was something in the way he looked at me that told of a hunger. I also felt that he and Damon did not have the same closeness that twins reputedly do. Furthermore, one day when they were ten years old and I was nine, I had seen something that I could never forget.

It was a hand-to-hand combat training session run by the older boys in the agoge, the college where boys are schooled, living away from home from the age of seven. The girls often join them for these sessions, but they don't sleep there. I had been sent with a message for Pericles, the seventeen-year-old leader, when I arrived to find the close-combat session in full flow. Among the maybe thirty or so boys circling each other with wooden knives were Lysander and Damon. Only the knife that Lysander was holding was not made of wood. It glinted in the light, and the instructor hadn't noticed. He hadn't noticed me either, being preoccupied showing a combatant a particular move.

I ran to Lysander and wrenched the knife from his hand. He looked as if he had been shocked out of a trance, his face blank. I think he barely saw me. Damon slowly handed his brother his own wooden knife; then, to my utter amazement, he hugged him gently. What must have been in Lysander's mind that day, what his actual intentions were, I couldn't begin to guess. Maybe he didn't know what he was doing either. What stunned me just as much was Damon's reaction. As though he had no thought for his own safety. Only concern for his brother.

None of us said anything to anyone afterwards. But in trying to get to the roots of the incident, I did ask my father who Damon and Lysander were named after. He told me that Damon was the name of the admiral of the Spartan fleet that helped to defeat the Persians; he and Uncle Leon had served under him, and hugely respected his leadership and his care for his men. When I asked my father about Lysander, his face became troubled. He explained how

Uncle Leon's father, Lysander, had betrayed Lady Danae's first husband to his death in armed conflict. How Uncle Leon had wanted his other son named after Danae's father, not his, because of the shame. But she had insisted that the name should continue, in the way of tradition, saying that one terrible mistake should not cause a man to be forgotten forever. She also said that history cherishes the name of Lysander, as a famous Spartan general and admiral. All the same, I think Damon must have inherited his caring nature from his beautiful and kind mother. Whereas she and Uncle Leon must ask themselves at times what possesses their other son.

What's in a name? I think, an awful lot. But that is because of my namesake, whose memory powers me on towards my destiny. Is the name of Lysander tainted somehow? When I look into his hungry eyes, I wonder. And when, years later, I look into the eyes of the stranger whose gaze is devouring me and my Olympic gold, I see what I think is the same hunger.

TWO

'A MIGHTY WARRIOR'
The *Iliad*, Book 1

Not long after we've returned home from the Games, my father tells me that we have a visitor. He and Uncle Leon want both our families to receive a general who is also a king. This is not uncommon in Sparta, where girls and women are expected to attend important meetings, be outspoken, and have their words listened to. (Another aspect of Laconia that you won't find anywhere else in Greece.)

So, seated in the throne room when King Alexander of Macedon is announced, are the two Spartan kings and their families. My mother and Aunt Danae sit together, and I seat myself with Lysander and Damon. My father and theirs sit on two very ordinary wooden armchairs with some perfunctory carvings; these are thrones, Spartan-style. There are two grander thrones, inlaid with gold, but they are used only for state occasions.

The two kings are in their army crimson tunics and cloaks, and so are Lysander, Damon, and me. When King Alexander of Macedon enters, the men all stand and Uncle Leon offers him a chair. Bowing to the assembly, he says, if it will not inconvenience us, he would prefer to stand. He speaks as he walks, swiftly, and with a hint of impatience.

I look at the man whose gaze so transfixed me as I lined up with my teammates for my Olympic gold. And I have to concede that he's done well in the looks department. Not tall, but well-proportioned and muscular. The jut of his nose and the set of his lips tell of one who does not suffer fools gladly. The hair is dark and curling: short-cropped, unlike the flaxen locks of King Leon and his two sons. And, at this stage anyway, he's on a charm offensive; definitely preferable to his reputation as a warrior, who, though only two years older than Damon and Lysander, has never been defeated.

His speech is slightly rushed, as though his thoughts are flying at a speed faster than his words can keep up with. 'My ladies, your Majesties, and my noble masters, I thank you all for granting me this audience at such short notice. I come to you because of your bold and unstinting leadership in utterly defeating the latest Persian invasion that threatened all Greece. It is my mission, my crusade, to continue my father's work in conquering Persia, to take revenge for all these past invasions. In this mission, I have the support of the Corinthian League…' he pauses, 'of which Sparta is not a member.'

Uncle Leon says in his quiet voice, 'Surely our actions in defending Greece speak for themselves?'

'A MIGHTY WARRIOR'

Alexander has the grace to look slightly ashamed, and I wonder if he has the remotest idea that he is talking to the two generals who crushed the Persians. 'They do indeed, your Majesty. And I come to you to offer Sparta the opportunity to throw her might behind this crusade, as proof that she wishes to see the Persian threat annihilated once and for all.' He pauses again, and says, in a quieter voice, where the menace rolls like the early rumble of an earthquake, 'My allies in the Corinthian League appreciate the motto that those who are not with me are against me.'

I can see my father's knuckles whiten, as he grips the wooden arms of his throne. And I bite my lip hard. This is a blatant threat to a country that has offered Alexander of Macedon no harm. Alexander pauses for a third time but is met with silence. He continues, in a more placating tone of voice, 'I do not ask for Sparta's entire army, mighty combatants though they would be.' Now his eyes turn to me. 'I have had the pleasure of watching your female mounted archers deal out resounding defeats in the Games. They are the weapons I ask for. If they join me in my conquest of Persia, I promise to let your time-honoured way of life here continue unchanged.'

The silence, when the youth called King Alexander of Macedon has finished speaking, is deafening. I truly believe that my father is speechless with rage. Then Uncle Leon stands, his quiet voice calm. 'Sir, if you had taken the trouble to acquaint yourself with our "time-honoured way of life", you would know that this is not a decision that can be made by Sparta's kings. You will need to meet with the ephors, who decide all foreign policy matters.'

I AM LYDIA

The curling lips tighten. 'When can I do that?'

Uncle Leon's voice must sound annoyingly relaxed to this man who is so used to imposing his will on others. 'You will be notified. In the meantime, we can offer you and your retinue accommodation in our barracks.'

I suppress a smile. I'll bet that the members of the Corinthian League offered rather fancier lodgings when Alexander came calling. Taken aback, although probably not for very long, he allows himself and his men to be escorted to the barracks. As soon as he's out of the room, I say what needs to be said: 'The Myrmidons will go with him. It's the only way to keep him off Sparta's back!'

My father growls, 'That would be cowering at the bludgeoning of a bully!'

I go over to him and sit at his feet. It's what I've always done when I need to get my own way. 'Dearest Father, think about the advantages! We can get intelligence on what this warmonger is doing. I can communicate through the mounted division of the Krypteia, just like you did when you were spying on the Persians.'

Uncle Leon says, 'Your daughter has a point, brother. Look how well intelligence served us at that time.' Some backstory here: my father and Uncle Leon are not biological brothers but definitely blood brothers, from all the fighting they've done together and the times when each saved the other's life. So right from when I first learned to talk, King Leon told me to always call him Uncle.

Lysander stands suddenly. 'I'll go too, Father!'

Uncle Leon says gently, 'And risk your life as well?'

'It would demonstrate Sparta's commitment to

Alexander's "crusade", as he calls it. And, as Lydia says, help to keep him off Sparta's back.'

Aunt Danae says warmly, 'That is a brave offer, Lysander.' She turns to her husband. 'And it is right that both our families commit to this enterprise.'

Uncle Leon bows to his wife. 'In that case, my lady, Lysander will be supported to the hilt.' My father says that Uncle Leon continues to call his wife 'my lady' long after they were married, because he simply worships her. I think that is beautiful.

Uncle Leon turns to Lysander. 'You will go with a cohort of fifty cavalry, the same in number as the Myrmidons. But you must promise to care for their welfare as if they were your own family.'

Lysander bows to his father. 'I promise, Father.'

I think that Lysander's offer has a hidden agenda. But at least it'll keep him away from Damon. I say to my father with a touch of irony, 'And the meeting with the ephors?'

He looks at Uncle Leon and back at me. 'Let's just say that your uncle and I have a special relationship with the ephors. In military affairs, they know they can trust us.'

*

When the decision is communicated to Alexander the next morning, he's impressed that he's getting more than he asked for. It is arranged that Lysander and I, with our troops, will meet up with the Macedonian army at Pella, their capital. Father says that he will organise a baggage train that will get us as far as Pella. Alexander has promised that, beyond

Pella, his own supply chains will keep us furnished with all that we need to eat, fight, and feed our horses. He has undertaken to run a regular supply line to Spartan forges, to collect consignments of the Myrmidons' special arrows. He will also pay us mercenaries the same rate as his regular army.

Uncle Leon, meanwhile, has been in close conversation with Erebos, the current leader of the Krypteia. Alexander doesn't know it, but his army is going to be shadowed and reported on through every step of their campaign in Persia. I will be informing my team about the codes and protocols that will be used when a meeting with Erebos is needed.

Then, Uncle Leon invites me to ride out with him for a briefing on everything he knows about Alexander of Macedon: information garnered during his time as leader of the Krypteia. I wonder why Lysander isn't part of this; towards the end of our conversation, I find out.

Riding Arion and Peg, we walk in a leisurely way along the lower slopes of Mount Taygetos, as the sun clears the horizon and the day becomes warmer. Uncle Leon's blue eyes are reflective, as he begins: 'Without his father's achievements, Alexander would be in no position to take on Persia. Philip the Second succeeded in uniting the different peoples of his country, making Macedon the powerful overlord of all the great Greek states, except Sparta.'

'That's the Corinthian League he was talking about?'

'Correct.'

'Was Alexander well educated, Uncle?'

'Brought up on a diet of Homer and the teachings of Aristotle. He carries with him a text of the *Iliad* specially prepared for him by Aristotle. He lives off the Homeric ideal; sees himself as "a mighty warrior". And wants to continue his father's work by conquering all of Persia. He first led troops to war at sixteen.'

'A precocious teenager.'

'Two years later, at Chaeronea, against the combined Theban and Athenian army, Alexander destroyed the Thebans' elite Sacred Band in a single, headlong cavalry charge.'

We stop to let the horses drink from a stream. 'His father was murdered, wasn't he?'

'Going foolishly unarmed to his daughter's wedding, he was stabbed by a traitorous bodyguard. As Alexander had quarrelled recently with his father over a recent marriage Philip had made, there were some who assumed he was complicit.'

I'm seeing Lysander and the glinting knife, circling his brother. 'What do you think, Uncle?'

'In Greek countries other than Sparta, the sword has always spoken more mightily than the law, Liddy. And Alexander was contending with other prospective heirs to the throne of Macedon.'

'So I'm fighting for someone who is completely ruthless about winning battles of all kinds; sounds like a good side to be on.'

We walk the horses on past the stream. Uncle Leon says, 'We have no reports that he treats his men badly. But his whole style is reckless, very powerful, deeply personal and extremely fast. And that, I think, is why he wants you and your Myrmidons.'

I AM LYDIA

'Break the enemy line before it has even properly formed? Our proposition for Sparta's army?'

'Exactly. And now,' Uncle Leon's voice has changed to a softer note, 'I want you to tell me why you think Lysander has not been involved in this conversation.'

'Because the next thing you are going to say to me is something he mustn't hear?'

Uncle Leon looks at me closely, his voice still very gentle. 'Do you know the real reason why Lysander has volunteered for this mission?'

'He… has another agenda. I think I know that.'

Uncle Leon halts Arion and Peg stops obediently. His voice is even quieter than usual as his blue eyes seek mine. 'You are the agenda, Liddy. He is coming to be near you. He is so in love with you that it is eating him up.'

'I… that's not good for him, is it?'

'No. I have known for a long time.'

'Because you can get into people's heads, can't you, Uncle?'

'You're good at that yourself, Liddy. You saw something, didn't you? When you were nine? The hand-to-hand combat training?'

'I took the knife from him. But Damon knew.'

'He sees Damon as a rival for your affections. Damon knows that, too. It was he who asked me to talk to you about it.'

Now I struggle for words. 'Damon asked you, Uncle?'

'He has the same ability to understand what someone is feeling and thinking. He loves his brother; he can feel his suffering.'

'A MIGHTY WARRIOR'

I have never felt so confused or so helpless. There's a long pause before I say, 'But what can I do about this, Uncle?'

'Look upon him with eyes that do not see the knife. Treat him as a fellow Spartan soldier. It could ease his pain a little.' There are tears in Uncle Leon's eyes. 'I hesitate to ask this of you, Liddy, but I am deeply worried about Lysander. I fear there is some fate hanging over him.'

'Could Damon not have asked me himself?'

'If Lysander even suspected that his brother had been alone and talking with you, it would have lashed his torment further.'

'Of course. I'm an idiot.'

Uncle Leon nudges Arion into a walk and we turn for home. 'This is terribly unfair on you, Liddy.'

'I hate to think of him suffering! I'll do what I can. But I have no idea what love is. And it would be cruel to give him false hope!'

'Yes. It would be very dangerous to do that.'

*

When I tell the Myrmidon team leaders that King Alexander of Macedon wants us to help spearhead his conquest of Persia, there is a cheer. Trained to a peak of battle fitness, and with Olympic golds under their belt, they had been longing for some action. Immediately, we set about checking our weapons, our armour and that of our horses, examining their physical condition, and ensuring that plenty of fodder is aboard the supply train. Aunt Danae kindly offers us some back-up mounts in case of accident or lameness. My father says that Alexander has promised to keep our cavalry mounted from his animals; we prefer to take our own spares.

And so, on a bright morning, with a warm wind blowing the dust from under the hooves of our convoy, we set off for the Macedonian capital of Pella. There are no emotional farewells; that's not the way Spartans do things. But the night before, my father gave me the gift of his own sword that he had forged himself; with the silver engraving of a wolf's head in the hilt, it is as beautiful as it is deadly. From time to time, I rest my hand on it and draw strength from its cool weight.

Embedded in the cavalry's ranks are ten Krypteian officers, two of whom ride ahead as scouts and two behind as guards. And, mindful of my conversation with Uncle Leon, I ride much of the time with Lysander. At first, he seems stunned to see me join him; then his tongue-tied shyness gradually thaws. And I notice that he and Damon are not really identical twins at all. To begin with, Lysander's eyes are the brilliant blue of his father's, while Damon's are more grey-blue. Lysander's hair is a paler flaxen colour than his brother's. And although both are strong and competent cavalrymen, Lysander is not quite as muscular as Damon. He also smiles only seldom; unlike his brother, who bestows smiles as the sun does its rays, like his beautiful mother.

I wonder if I can do something about this dearth of smiles. So I recount to Lysander all that Uncle Leon has told me about Alexander's education and achievements from a very young age, concluding, 'He lacks nothing in self-confidence, either; some say that he considers himself of divine race. They say he even has a habit of casting his eyes upwards and to the right, as if he were constantly communing with some unseen presence.'

For the first time I've ever seen, Lysander laughs. 'That must make him look ridiculous!'

'It does! His father must have been pretty pompous too. He once threatened us, "If I enter Laconia with my army successfully, I will raze Sparta to the ground." Guess what the Spartan reply was? Suitably laconic, of course.'

With a smile that makes his blue eyes glow brightly, Lysander promptly replies, '*If!*' And I realise that, far from this being hard work, I am greatly enjoying his company.

*

When we reach Pella, the whole city is teaming with the Macedonian army and the preparations for war on Persia. But I'm impressed by the way that Alexander welcomes me and Lysander with our forces, and introduces us to the leaders of his fifteen thousand-strong phalanx. The Spartans can do powerful phalanxes, but that of the Macedonians is even more formidable, because of their eighteen-foot-long spears, called sarissas. These spears are a great deal longer than the ones we Spartans use, and I can see Lysander taking good note of this.

Alexander explains to his commanders how the Myrmidons have the edge on speed and can smash enemy front lines with their archery, and how Lysander's highly trained cavalry can back up theirs in harrying and outflanking. This all gets a favourable reaction. So, by the time we settle for the night, well fed from Alexander's supply train, and with our horses tended to, we Spartans are in a good frame of mind.

While Alexander and his top commanders sleep in tents, my troops and Lysander's wrap themselves in their cloaks and rest near their horses. I stand guard at a good distance from the Macedonian sentries on watch, until I see a pinpoint of light flash three times from deep in the surrounding darkness. And I know that Erebos is not far away. Lysander knows nothing of this. He has enough to deal with. My heart aches with pity for him.

*

We set off on the journey to Persia in the early hours of the morning, in an endless column. The Myrmidons – at Alexander's orders – are close to the front. Two hours into the journey, Lysander rides up alongside me. He has been talking to the Macedonian commanders and gained a great deal of useful information. 'A vanguard of Alexander's army is already established across the Bosphorus on the shore of Asia Minor. His father sent it there two years ago, under the veteran General Parmenio. They have occupied several of the Greek-populated cities of the coast.'

'Have they taken on the local Persians?'

'A few skirmishes and some minor setbacks; but so far no major engagement.'

'Do you know what our combined strength will be when we join them?'

'Seventeen thousand infantry and five thousand cavalry.'

'So Alexander will be looking for a scrap with Darius?'

'Not Darius – not yet, anyway. The local Persian commander is called Memnon. Apparently, we will be fairly evenly matched in numbers. But first, Alexander intends to call at Troy.'

'To pay homage to his Homeric heroes, I suppose?'

'And to sacrifice to the gods. Oh, and Memnon himself is actually Greek, as are his infantry.'

'This is going to feel weird – Greek fighting Greek to conquer Persia!'

There is something in Lysander's eyes that I realise is pity. 'And sadly, not unusual. So many fighting men were left landless and masterless after all the past battles, that we will always be up against our own kind. But Alexander aims to go for Persians over Greeks every time, and the first line is likely to be Persian cavalry.'

I look at Lysander with a new respect. He speaks like a seasoned military commander, even though he is so new to this. And he has been taking the trouble to inform himself as well as he can about what we will be facing.

I think back to my many conversations with my father. 'The Persians don't fight as well as the Greeks. They just don't have the appetite for it.'

Lysander's blue eyes flash with anger. 'Little wonder, when they're treated like dogs. The Persians just rely on numbers and have no care for the men they send into battle.'

Uncle Leon must have been schooling his son thoroughly; this is almost word for word what my father has told me. How the Persian soldiers' armour is no match for

Spartan arrows. How the Persians haven't even been trained to swim; so many thousands of them lost their lives in the naval battle in the Gulf of Corinth. If they could just have swum to shore, all that would have awaited them would have been slavery. I remember Uncle Leon's instructions to his son, to look after his men like family, and I'm beginning to believe that is exactly what this young commander will do. I'd better make sure that I show equal care for my Myrmidons.

*

I find that my quick-witted troops have been making observations of their own on this trek towards the coast. Trotting beside me on Apollo, Penelope has some interesting insights as to Alexander's supply train: 'Have you noticed that there are no ox-drawn carts? Only pack animals – horses, donkeys, and camels. And the soldiers are marching carrying up to a month's supply of flour each!'

I laugh. 'Catch your Athenian citizen deigning to do without porters as he goes to war!'

Penelope continues, 'But that's what's making us so fast. Ox-drawn carts slow everyone down.'

I start to use my head at last. 'So this could be one of the reasons why Alexander always wins a fight. He gets there so quickly, the other side just aren't ready?'

Penelope nods. 'That's why he wants us. We're fast, too. The best. Oh, and I've taken a look at the Macedonian arrowheads.'

'How did you do that?'

She taps her nose. 'Never you mind, boss. Anyway, they're made of iron, but with only two lobes and just one of the lobes nicked. And the bowman who showed me his arrows also told me about the Persians.'

Now I have to laugh. 'Pen, what kind of deal was this? I'll show you mine if you show me yours?'

With a grin, she taps her nose again and says, 'The Persians are still using bronze arrowheads. And javelins with fire-hardened wood for points.'

'And probably still as poorly armoured as they were when my father and Uncle Leon took them on in the last war?'

Penelope bashes a horrible-looking fly off Apollo's neck. 'Even the Macedonians don't have bronze armour like we do. It's layers of glazed linen. Their horses are nowhere near as well protected as ours, either.'

'Nice one, Pen. And did you show this Macedonian bowman your arrows?'

She grins again, slightly more wickedly this time. 'I gave him one, as a little thank-you.'

THREE
'TO DEAL OUT DEATH AMONG HEROES'
The *Iliad*, Book 16

A week later, we cross the Hellespont, in sixty ships which are the backbone of Alexander's small navy. With an army our size, it takes many crossings, and three weeks. It's a narrow strait, but it means something huge to Alexander. Here he is, entering seriously on his campaign – his 'crusade', as he puts it – to subdue the vast realms of Persia. Already the overlord of most of Greece, he now seeks to bring the King of Kings under his heel.

As we land in the first ships with Alexander, he throws himself ahead of everyone into the water and flings his spear into the sand of the beach. Next to me, Lysander comments, 'He is signifying that he has received Asia from the gods as a spear-won prize.'

'TO DEAL OUT DEATH AMONG HEROES'

Rather acidly, I reply, 'Let's hope the gods are looking!' And it's sweet to hear Lysander laugh quietly; he's smiling and laughing a lot more now.

Before Alexander brings Memnon and his army of mercenaries to battle, he has a visit to make. Troy is, fittingly, the first city he intends to liberate from Persian domination. He expects a warm welcome, and he wants me and my Myrmidons, and Lysander and his cohort, to accompany him. So while the rest of the army takes a break, we gallop with him to Homer's 'windy city'. My father told me how close he came to Troy on his epic pre-emptive strike initiative with Uncle Leon, when their modest cohort dealt massive damage to the Persians' three hundred thousand-strong army. The thought of seeing a place that has dwelled for so long only in my imagination makes me tingle with excitement.

In the second Persian invasion of Greece, Xerxes is said to have sacrificed a thousand oxen at Troy, before crossing the Hellespont in the opposite direction from us. He would have made the sacrifice at the temple of Athena, patron goddess of the city; the temple is still there, with its simple architecture and slender columns. And there is the tomb of Achilles, the mighty warrior born of a goddess mother, Thetis, and mortal father, the Greek king, Peleus. Next to Achilles' tomb is that of Patroclus, his loving and loyal friend, who was killed in battle after he bravely took Achilles' place, wearing his armour. Temple and tombs are surrounded by a few dwellings; but of the city walls of Troy in its grandeur, of the palace that housed the noble Hector and his wife and child, nothing remains.

I AM LYDIA

With the few hundred Trojans who have come out to applaud the arrival of their deliverer looking on, we troops line up and salute as Alexander offers sacrifice to Athena. In memory of all the heroes who are buried here, he solemnly pours libations of wine to the parched ground. Then he makes a gift of his armour to the temple and takes, in exchange, the finest of the suits of armour that were hanging on the temple walls, still preserved from the Trojan war.

I mutter to Lysander, 'Is that really a fair exchange? He's not a legend like Achilles, is he?'

He whispers back, 'No, but he yearns to be. This is the story of his life.' I soon realised how right Lysander was. Alexander wore the ancient armour at his first battle, and it was still with him nine years and many thousands of miles later.

Then we watch as Hephaestion, Alexander's favourite, lays a wreath on the tomb of Patroclus. In turn, Alexander lays a wreath on Achilles' tomb. So he and his most trusted friend are directly comparing themselves with Homer's heroes. The overlord of most of Greece announces over the tomb, 'Achilles, you are a lucky man! You have had, while you lived, the most faithful of friends. And when you died, you had Homer to proclaim your deeds and preserve your memory. Would that I could have so eloquent a witness!' To round it all off, in accordance with tradition, he and Hephaestion then have a naked running race around the temple.

I throw a sideways look at Lysander. 'Is that why he brought us here? To be his eloquent witnesses?'

His blue eyes have a spark of mischief. 'I can't write poetry. Can you?'

'TO DEAL OUT DEATH AMONG HEROES'

'I could try. But it would be rubbish.'

'So let's stick to what we're good at, shall we?'

I really want to ask Lysander what he thinks we're good at when the gallop back to camp is called. And so begins Alexander's conquest of Persia.

*

That night, I sneak out of the camp for a brief conference with Erebos, who has been gathering information on the deliberations of the Persians, now that they are aware of the arrival of the Macedonian upstart, as they see Alexander.

'The Persians held a council of local satraps to discuss strategy. Memnon, Darius' Greek commander, advocated a scorched-earth policy.'

'I bet that didn't go down too well.'

'Nothing that Memnon suggests goes down too well, because he's Greek. But the satraps didn't want their crops, farms, and villages burned.'

'They'll stand and fight?'

He nods. 'At the River Granicus. It's roughly sixty feet wide, with a fast current and steep embankments.'

'So we provide cover while he gets his men across. There'll be a hail of javelins and Persian archer fire.'

'But not static cover, or you'll become targets too.'

'Definitely on-the-move cover. Any more information on numbers?'

'The Persians are big on cavalry – ten thousand versus Alexander's five thousand. But they won't be able to use their scythed chariots on those slippery riverbanks.'

'Infantry?'

'Five thousand Greek mercenaries, versus your seventeen thousand Macedonians.'

'Thank you, Erebos.'

*

The next day, I brief the girls as we begin the march to the River Granicus. Then I slip back to Lysander's cohort and let him in on the news. He's known for a while about the Krypteia shadowing us and the Persians; as I saw him becoming more relaxed, I felt that it was time to open up. He says that the Macedonian commanders have scouts reporting back that the Persians are on their way to the river.

'Wonder who'll get there first?'

He steadies his horse as it stamps a hoof at a particularly vicious insect bite. 'General Parmenio wanted to attack tomorrow morning. But Alexander said it would "disgrace the Hellespont should he fear the Granicus". We should be there by the afternoon; he reckons it'll all be over in an hour.'

'And presumably, he wants us to provide cover while you're in the water?'

'Yes. Repeated, very fast shock-and-awe charges.'

When we get to the River Granicus, the Persian army is waiting for us. It's a baffling sight. Xanthippe murmurs, 'What do they think they're doing? They've boxed their cavalry in!'

As Lysander had predicted, the ten thousand-strong Persian cavalry is in the front line, with the five thousand

'TO DEAL OUT DEATH AMONG HEROES'

Greek mercenaries behind them. But this is not the place to put your cavalry in the front. They can neither move forward because of the steep riverbank, nor pull back because of the location of the infantry. However, that's their problem.

We Myrmidons take formation on the right flank, where Alexander has said he wants us. He has made himself extremely conspicuous by the large white plume on his helmet and the brightly polished suit of ancient armour that he has brought with him from Troy. I can guess why; he is aware that the Persians are not afraid of him, because they don't know him. After this battle, he intends that their ignorance will have turned to fear. Around him are his eight bodyguards, his elite Companion Cavalry forces – in which he has now included Lysander and his cohort – and his light troops stationed on the far right. The crushing force of the Macedonian phalanx with its eighteen-foot sarissas awaits the light javelins of the Persians.

For a brief moment, the fast-flowing river between them, both armies stand in silence. Then, to the sound of trumpets and war cries, Alexander leads the advance into the water. We hurl ourselves into the first of many shock-and-awe charges, galloping to the bank, firing deadly blasts across the water into their poorly armoured troops, and veering sharply away at high speed, before they can fire back. It's clear that the Persians were not expecting Alexander to charge across precisely where their line appeared strongest, and it's also plain that they were not expecting the storms of lethal iron-barbed arrows that the Myrmidons are hurling at them.

They respond with a shower of arrows and javelins, intent on attacking our men in the water, where the footing is slippery and difficult. We can see Memnon himself leading the Persian centre. And I imagine that, right now, their sole aim is to kill Alexander. They come close. In the first charge, he loses that white-plumed helmet crest to a blow that would have cleaved through his skull, had he not been helmeted. In the second, his horse is killed beneath him (not the magnificent Bucephalus, but tragic all the same).

But he's planned this well, plunging into the water and up the opposite bank diagonally, in order to encounter the foe as far as possible in a broad line of attack rather than a column. And with the loss of a number of their leaders, due to the headlong energy of Alexander's commanders and Myrmidon arrows, the Persians are becoming disorganised, and their morale is plummeting. Soon, the Persian cavalry that so outnumbers ours is in disarray and streaming to the back.

And now, we come to a part of the battle which I can only remember with shame. Throughout the struggle so far, the Greek mercenary infantry remained in its position and did not move. As the Persians fell back, Alexander, instead of pursuing the retreating troops as you might have expected, turned his attention instead to the mercenaries. This completely contradicted what Lysander had told me, about Alexander planning to focus on the Persians and not the Greeks.

Having done nothing to attack him, they pleaded for mercy. But, whether he was annoyed at nearly having had his head cut off, or because he detested Greeks who took Persian money to fight Greeks, or because his judgement was not that good in his first major battle with the Persians,

'TO DEAL OUT DEATH AMONG HEROES'

Alexander gave no mercy to these experienced, desperate men. Because they were extremely good fighters, who he could have recruited to his own ranks with great benefit, he lost more of his own soldiers than in the entire battle before taking on the Greek mercenaries. It was completely unnecessary, bloody slaughter. Of the five thousand Greek mercenaries, only two thousand survived; they were sent to Macedon to work the mines.

The Myrmidons return to camp with no one saying a word. I feel so sickened by this gratuitous blood-letting that I can't force food into my mouth. I can see Alexander doing the rounds, visiting the wounded, listening to their stories, and lining up various heroes for medals. He also buries Greeks and Persians alike; although, Lysander says, the Persians normally prefer to burn their dead. But there were many heroes who did not need to be dealt death to. Three thousand Greek warriors. Whatever else Alexander is going to do during his conquest of Persia, we are never going to forget this.

*

When I visit Lysander later that evening, he's bandaging a thigh wound for one of his men and talking to him in a low voice. He looks up. 'This couldn't wait for the medics.'

I pass the soldier my flask of water. 'If he had granted the Greek mercenaries quarter, our medics wouldn't be nearly as busy now.'

There's a quiet fury in Lysander's voice. 'Those men had no choice but to fight for the enemy to make a living. They had not raised a hand against us, either. If you are a good leader, when they ask for mercy, you give it; and they will put their lives on the line for you with ferocious loyalty.'

'Your father once said to me that Alexander's style was deeply personal; I think I'm beginning to understand what he meant.'

'Are your troops unscathed?'

'Physically, yes. But very angry with the brute they're fighting for.'

*

There follow some rest days, much needed because of the heavy toll of wounded. The Myrmidons support the hard-pressed medics; we all have a good knowledge of anatomy, and training in first aid. As we're dealing mainly with less serious injuries, it becomes quite a social occasion. Many of the Macedonian soldiers only realise at this point that the mounted archers, who downed so many of the Persian cavalry at the start of the battle, are actually female. There is much mutual admiration, comparison of weaponry, expeditions across camp to view mounts, and talk of mounted races when wounds have healed. Once, I see Penelope introducing Xanthippe to a strikingly handsome young man, who must be her informant about Macedonian and Persian arrows.

That evening, Macedonians and Myrmidons share food together in a most convivial atmosphere. I dine with Lysander, and I can see from his sombre expression that he's still horrified at the slaughter of the Greek mercenaries. He eats little; as I still have hardly any appetite, I suggest a stroll now that the worst heat of the sun is over. So we go and check the horses, then walk on into the shade of a nearby wood.

He says thoughtfully, 'Does what happened today make you think twice about following this man, Lydia?'

It's the first time he's used my name; the formality of it surprises me after our cosy, conspiratorial conversations at Troy. 'Yes. It came as a shock that he can be so murderously vindictive, and also show such poor judgement in both a military and a moral sense. And you, Lysander, how do you feel?' I think, if you're trying out my name, I'll do the same with yours. I find I like saying his name.

He is frowning as he weighs my question in the balance. 'I feel duty-bound to be loyal to him, although it sticks in my throat for all your reasons. And apart from the dishonour of quitting when we have barely begun, Alexander has left behind a force of twelve thousand infantry and fifteen hundred cavalry in Greece. Enough to make Sparta pay a heavy price if we desert.'

'Standing alone and apart from all the Greek states that are in the League of Corinth, she could expect no help from them, either.'

'So, we have answered the question, have we not?' His tone is suddenly lighter; he smiles at me, and my mood lifts too. It means that our journey together can continue, at least until Alexander has completed his crusade in Persia. By then, perhaps, Lysander and I might be looking forward to a longer journey together. It means that the pleasure I derive from his company will not suddenly come to an end; unless one of us is killed, or both of us are.

FOUR

DAYS OF SIEGE AND THUNDER

I don't see Lysander for the whole of the next day, as he's tied up in discussions with Alexander and his commanders; it leaves me quite out of sorts. When I do see him again, the entire army is on the move southwards, with the Myrmidons in their usual place near the front. Xanthippe trots up beside me on Heracles and says, 'Any guesses as to what the plan is?'

'Well, southwards is not where Darius is; he's in the east. So I imagine that His Wonderfulness is planning to bring the port cities under his control and kick the Persian navy out of the Aegean.'

'Creating a big setback for Darius' supply line.'

At that moment, Lysander's handsome dark bay arrives on my other side. 'Correct. And we'll be up against Memnon again. Apparently, he's gathering another vast army.'

I say, 'Doubtless shored up with expendable Greek mercenaries?'

'As many as twenty thousand. But Memnon is holed up at Ephesus, further south; before that, we have to take Sardis.'

*

At first, Alexander's southwards campaign looks almost too easy. On receiving news of the approach of the Macedonian army, the Persian satrap at the inland city of Sardis, Mithrines, surrenders without a fight. Next, we march south-west for four days until we get to Ephesus. And here again, the Persian force – this one under Memnon – makes a hasty retreat rather than risk battle: result – minimal bloodshed, the kind of war we like. And here, to our great surprise, after his treatment of the Greek mercenaries at the Granicus, Alexander pardons even those citizens who had opposed him before his arrival. He restores democracy to the city and recalls Ephesians, who had been exiled by the Persians.

Two more strategically important cities are captured by detachments of the army. Then, one evening, Lysander joins me and the girls at supper. 'Our scouts have found the vast Persian force; it is gathering in the port city of Miletus. This is going to be nothing like as easy as we've had it so far.'

'A siege?'

He nods. 'Probably a protracted one. Miletus has a strong outer wall, and an inner section containing a second wall, and fortifications for the citadel. The Persian fleet in the Aegean is never far from its port, so the garrison at Miletus is well supplied and well informed.'

After we make camp outside Miletus, within sight of the blue Aegean, the good news goes round like wildfire. Alexander has discovered that the Persian fleet is out of port. He has ordered his admiral, Nicanor, to blockade the harbour of Miletus with his 160 Macedonian vessels. This is a masterstroke: Nicanor's little navy can render the far larger Persian force completely useless. A wonderful example, as my father says about the Persians, of when sheer numbers quickly become mere numbers.

With the Persian fleet barred from the harbour of Miletus, and Memnon's large army garrisoned inside the city walls, Alexander launches a siege. And I get to see one of the reasons why he has this reputation as unbeatable. It was actually his father, Philip of Macedon, who recognised the huge potential of the torsion catapult siege engine and commissioned a number of them. The torsion catapult is the successor to the single-armed catapult; rather than hurling missiles, it fires them like very large and powerful arrows, using a torsion spring. The torsion principle requires tightly wound fibres being drawn to a notched pull, similar to how a bow and arrow works. The projectiles are known as bolts; they are long and heavy – up to 170 pounds – and very accurate. Most commonly, the catapults fire missiles weighing from thirty to sixty pounds, from a distance of two thousand feet; this wall-penetrating power, and their high level of accuracy, has been a game-changer for military commanders, and Alexander is a big fan.

DAYS OF SIEGE AND THUNDER

Things are going well at first: the outer wall crumbles under constant bombardment from the siege engines. However, at around the same time, Persian naval reinforcements arrive, and Alexander has to siphon vital forces away from the main siege to boost Nicanor's blockade. This works; despite several attempts to lure our ships from their strong position, the mighty Persian navy is stuck with watching the remainder of the siege of Miletus helplessly from a distance.

So, with the Myrmidons providing covering arrow fire for the siege engines, our troops pound away at the damaged defences of Miletus. It's horrible work for them, with showers of missiles being hurled from the citadel walls and frequent counter-attacks launched by Memnon.

At one stage, the beleaguered citizens of Miletus have had enough; they don't particularly care for Persians or Macedonians. So a leading aristocrat named Glaucippas visits our camp and advises Alexander that the Milesians wish for there to be an end to hostilities. No prizes for guessing how the boss responds. While Glaucippas goes away to prepare his people for a lengthy siege, Alexander orders the construction of more siege engines, and the battering of the city walls goes on. And on.

After many days, the inner walls of the city finally give way, and there's a mass advance of our infantry to kick the remaining defenders out of the city. They don't succeed in catching the top dogs, though; Memnon and his command staff somehow manage to slip out unharmed and leg it southwards to Halicarnassus, their last retreat. A great many Persians and Greek mercenaries have a far worse fate. Some flee by floating into the harbour on makeshift rafts, or even shields; and sadly, most of them drown. To do him credit, Alexander grants amnesty to the remaining Milesians and – catch this – he even welcomes three hundred of Memnon's Greek mercenaries into our ranks. Artemisia mutters, 'Do you think he's learning to do the decent thing at last?'

*

If we thought that Miletus was a tough call, we had a real eye-opener coming with Halicarnassus. It's the greatest city in Caria, the region where we've been campaigning. It stretches across the Gulf of Cos and is extremely powerfully defended. The battlements have been extensively strengthened and form probably the most massive walls and towers of any city in the western Persian Empire.

As for the moat, it's forty feet wide and more than twenty feet deep, going right round the entire city. The outer defences enclose three immensely strong citadels; the two strongest, Salmacis and Arconnesus, are positioned either side of the harbour. Where, guess what, the Persian fleet sailed in to guarantee a great line of supply for the defenders, who number around thirty thousand. The least massively strong points (the word 'weak' just does not apply with this monster) are the three gates: immensely robust, and well guarded and maintained.

We set up camp about half a mile south-east of the city, and immediately, Alexander goes on the offensive. He orders the first assaults on the western gate, the Mylasa. We provide an advance charge ahead of the cavalry, with a hail of arrows to drive back the Persian skirmishers who come out to meet us. The cavalry bears down on them, they dive back inside, the gate slams shut, and it's game over for that day.

Over the next few days, the infantry intensifies its attacks on the city walls. Sappers begin to fill in that huge moat, and the lumbering siege engines arrive, with nothing to do until the moat is filled in. As at Miletus, the most we Myrmidons can do is provide cover for the siege engineers, and shock-and-awe charges for the cavalry, if skirmishers come out to take us on. And once again, punishing missile weapons are raining down from the walls. We all know that Alexander likes to get things over with quickly, but that is obviously not going to happen with Halicarnassus. The pounding of the walls goes on for days, with little apparent result.

Then our gallant sappers have completed the filling-in of the moat; with a solid footing now available, the siege engines prepare for an assault. If you're thinking, hurrah, they're going to smash it – don't bother. Because Halicarnassus has the most determined and creative defence imaginable. Once night falls, the Macedonian army makes the mistake of going to bed. Which is when a Persian patrol wreaks the kind of havoc that my father and Uncle Leon once did with the advancing Persian army: they infiltrate our lines and set fire to the siege equipment.

This is a horrible shock for Alexander, who had been expecting this kind of surprise as little as the Persians were, when my father and Uncle Leon, with their elite early strike force, came out of the night at them from the mountains. Once he's got out of bed, he manages to organise a counter-attack. But it costs us 316 casualties and huge damage to the siege engines. So days are lost, while we repair soldiers and equipment.

I'm helping Lysander with a leg wound that one of his men has sustained; it's deep and bloody, and the poor man has passed out with the pain. I say, 'We need a tourniquet to stem the bleeding.' Lashing the strips of linen tightly around the man's thigh, I mutter, 'I wish we had some yarrow; it's good for bleeding, and it's a disinfectant, too.'

Lysander says, 'What does it look like?'

'Little and white; have you read your *Iliad*?'

He nods.

'You'll find it at the end of Book 11. It's also called the Achilles herb.'

'I might have seen some growing beneath the battlements…' Before I can say a word, he's disappeared into the night. I wait with some trepidation, hoping that they're not still chucking missiles from the walls in addition to raiding the besieging camp. He's back in twenty minutes with the precious yarrow.

'That is brilliant!' I pour some water over the delicate little plant to clean off the dust and crush it by rubbing it between my hands. Then I apply it gently to the wound, quoting from the *Iliad*, where Patroclus removes an arrow from Eurypylus' thigh: '*this was a virtuous herb which killed all pain: so the wound presently dried and the blood left off flowing*'.

Lysander looks on. 'Why is it called the Achilles herb?'

'Patroclus uses it to treat an arrow wound in the *Iliad*, but he only knows about it because of Achilles. Achilles used it to treat the wounds of his men.'

'Your father used to be an armourer and a surgeon, didn't he?'

'He was the one who trained me.'

'My father told me that your father saved his life by amputating his lower leg, when it was crushed and badly infected.'

'He taught me how to do amputations, too. But this soldier will keep his leg, thanks to you!' And leaning across to Lysander, I kiss him on the lips. Trust me when I say that I have never kissed a man before. For a beginner, it's quite a long kiss, because once I've started, I don't want to stop, his lips are so tender and giving.

When I do stop, reluctantly, my heart pounding hammer blows, he gazes at me as though he's been hit by a lightning bolt, his blue eyes very bright. He whispers, 'I didn't know that finding a little herb in the middle of the night would bring me this.'

The soldier stirs slightly in his return to consciousness. I whisper to Lysander, 'You may have saved this man's life.'

'And you have saved mine, my lady.' He gets up.

'Where are you going?'

'To find some more yarrow. We need a plentiful supply of the Achilles herb!'

*

The siege dragged on, with the same repetitive pattern of our troops attacking and the Persians repairing and counter-attacking. Our army was becoming fatigued and difficult to control. One night, a number of troops, under the command of one Perdiccas, got drunk and made a mindless charge at the Mylasa gate. The Persians seized on this with glee and rushed outside to take them on. The skirmish rapidly escalated into a full-blown engagement, with Perdiccas bringing reinforcements and the Persians sending out more defenders. They soon outnumbered our troops, and yet more siege equipment was set alight. Only when Alexander appeared on the scene with additional troops did the Persians retire through the gate of the citadel. Alexander negotiated a brief truce with Memnon, for the many dead and wounded to be retrieved from below the city walls. And I was glad that Lysander had gathered a good supply of yarrow.

For more than a month, our forces had thundered away at the defences of Halicarnassus with little to show for it. The hot, dry summer was fading into autumn, and still the defenders fought back. To our dismay, some of the repaired sections of wall were even stronger than the originals. We could imagine what was going through Alexander's mind. The success of his entire expedition was being jeopardised; his prestige in the eyes of both Persians and Greeks was at stake. With the defenders well supplied by sea, he had no hope of starving them out, and no navy to take on theirs; what few of his ships remained, he had sent home from Miletus. But he could not afford to leave a key enemy stronghold alive and kicking on his western flank.

One day, the command goes through the ranks to prepare for a mass attack on the main gate of the city. This time, our forces are definitely threatening to penetrate the walls. We Myrmidons wait for the counter-attack and let fly as soon as the Persians appear through the massive gate. A pitched battle ensues in the shadow of the gate, in which the mighty Macedonian phalanxes are gaining the advantage. Then disaster strikes, as the retreating defenders cram together on the bridge of the moat, and it suddenly collapses under the weight. Many soldiers are killed.

Alexander's judgement is thankfully operating here on the side of humanitarianism. While he could have pushed through this success, he did not want to risk a slaughter inside the walls. I think he may still have had a faint hope that the citizens of Halicarnassus would pressure Memnon into a surrender. And as it was, around one thousand defenders and forty of our men were killed, some of them Alexander's most trusted officers.

In response, the Persians launched another night attack, this time a massive and carefully co-ordinated one. Some two thousand infantrymen were led by a Greek mercenary officer called Ephialtes on this raid, half of them being directed to fire the siege engines and the other half raiding our camp. We should have been better prepared for this, having been caught out at night before. Alexander organised the best of his infantrymen into three phalanxes and sent more crews to deal with the burning siege equipment. On foot, he took his place at the head of the formation, and advanced on Ephialtes.

It was a dire situation: lethal missiles were raining down from the city walls and from a one hundred-foot-high wooden tower that had been specially constructed for the raid. And for once, Alexander's charismatic leadership failed us; the Macedonians could not gain an advantage. When the phalanxes began to falter, Memnon rushed out of the gate with additional troops. And we all thought that a miracle was needed to prevent everything ending very badly indeed.

A miracle was what we got. It came from men who had long served under Alexander's father, King Philip the Second of Macedon. These veterans were exempt from combat duty under Alexander but still accompanied the army. Suddenly, these astonishing old soldiers appeared on the scene and, with a dramatic flair that rivalled Alexander himself, rallied the infantry with thunderous calls to arms. Freshly energised, the phalanxes tightened their ranks and surged forwards in an irresistible wave against Ephialtes' force. The massive power behind the eighteen-foot sarissas prevailed, with men going down in their hundreds, including Ephialtes. Memnon ordered a full retreat, and the city walls were penetrated before Alexander called off the pursuit, in another move ruled by prudence and good judgement.

Lysander put it nicely when he said it was the veterans who had snatched victory from the jaws of defeat. That extraordinary night battle was the turning point of a siege that had dragged on for more than two months. The defenders had held all the cards: Memnon's men were well supplied, they outnumbered ours, and they were expert at rebuilding as fast as we knocked their walls down. But they could not succeed against the unrelenting onslaught of our army – and the last-ditch intervention of men who had served under Alexander's father. The morning after, Memnon called an assembly of his generals, who came to a majority decision: to abandon Halicarnassus, as they had done Miletus.

*

Memnon and most of his army escaped by sea to the nearby island of Cos, after setting fire to many buildings in Halicarnassus. Triumphantly leading us through those gates that had resisted our efforts for so long, Alexander issued a decree that the citizens should not be harmed, and he ordered crews to put out the fires.

The final months of that momentous first year with Alexander's army found us at last on the move once more, having subdued the remaining pockets of resistance in Caria. Alexander left a substantial force behind to capture the two strongest citadels of Salmacis and Arconnesus, either side of the harbour; and it has to be said that they held out for another year before throwing in the towel.

Meanwhile, we were marching along the southern coast to subdue hostile forces in Lycia, Pamphylia, and Cilicia. It was a real buzz to think that in Cilicia, I was in the territory where my father and Uncle Leon had pursued their brilliant pre-emptive-strike strategy against the vast Persian army.

Then came winter, and Alexander allowed some of his veterans and recently married soldiers to visit their home country. But Lysander and I exchanged uneasy glances when we found out that these furloughed men had also been instructed to recruit new levies, not just from Corinthian League members but also from the Peloponessus, which, of course, included Sparta. 'I can imagine the response that they'll get from my father!'

He nodded grimly. 'Alexander is tightening his grip on

his Greek empire; doesn't want them to think that while the cat's away…'

I only found out later, through Erebos, that no further demands had been made of Sparta. I jokingly remarked to Lysander, 'He obviously considers that he's getting good value for money from us!'

He smiled. 'The Myrmidons are widely praised by his generals. They feel that you give a real cutting edge to the cavalry.'

'And the fact that you are included in their counsels with Alexander says it all about you!'

He looked embarrassed. 'I think it's more about Sparta than me. He has a lingering respect for our fierce independence.'

'And our fierceness in battle!'

'Talking of battle, he's planning to resume his campaign against Darius after calling at Gordium.'

'What's waiting for him at Gordium? More tombs?'

That spark of mischief is back in Lysander's blue eyes. 'A mystery to unravel.'

As at Troy, Alexander wants Lysander and me and our cohorts to come with him to Gordium, while the rest of the army enjoys a well-earned rest just outside the city. It turns out that this is all part of Alexander's plan, to become a legend in his own lifetime. What is waiting for him at Gordium is an ancient wagon, with its yoke tied with a load of knots, all so tightly entangled that it's impossible to see how to undo them.

While we're riding there, Lysander explains, 'Apparently, the wagon once belonged to Gordius, the father of the celebrated King Midas.'

'He of the golden touch?'

'The same. An oracle has declared that any man who can unravel these elaborate knots is destined to become ruler of all Asia.'

'So Alexander couldn't "knot" call by, could he?'

Politely passing over my awful joke, Lysander just gives me another of his smiles, now as sunny and warm as his brother's.

A large crowd of onlookers has gathered as we line up our troops and salute, while Alexander wrestles with the mass of gnarled ropes aided by his best mate, Hephaestion. I whisper to Lysander, 'How long before he loses his temper and draws his sword?'

At that moment, Alexander is heard to exclaim, 'It makes no difference how they are loosed!' Hephaestion is urging him to give it a bit more time, but Alexander is having none of it. Whipping out his sword, he slices the Gordian knot in half with a single stroke.

A cheer goes up from the locals, who are obviously happy to accept that the young king has outsmarted the ancient puzzle and claimed his right to rule all Asia. That night, the city is rocked by a violent storm, with hours of flashing lightning and crashing thunder. Naturally, Alexander puts it about that this weather episode means the gods are very happy with the Gordian knot outcome. Well, he would say that, wouldn't he? When I discussed this with Lysander, we had to admire the boss's public-relations work. Alexander is a man who makes his own luck and carries all before him through a personality that is a force of nature.

FIVE

'I SHALL GO WHEREVER YOU ARE'

Alexander's first encounter with King Darius the Third of Persia had a beginning that was sickening and cowardly almost beyond belief. You may not be able to stomach this; in which case, skip the next bit. But it has to be told. On his way to bring Darius to battle at the River Penarus, Alexander left a number of sick and wounded soldiers to recover at the port town of Issus. Coming through Issus after Alexander had set up his base there, the Persian king tortured and executed our recuperating soldiers, and cut off the right hand of those who were allowed to live.

When our troops heard about this, their resolve to deal Darius a crushing defeat was white-hot. You could feel their anger in the air, like lightning before it strikes. As usual, we were heavily outnumbered; Darius had 140,000 men. But they were of many different tribes and languages, with a

'I SHALL GO WHEREVER YOU ARE'

corresponding lack of cohesiveness, whilst our troops were all Macedonians and Greeks, smouldering with a shared hatred of the cowardly Darius, who had dealt such cruelty to our sick and wounded at Issus.

In cold, rainy weather, the two armies confronted each other across the River Penarus. On the face of it, the Persian king was in a position of strength; he had arrived some thirty-six hours before we did and could choose where to fight from. However, Darius' choice of position had the same effect of restricting his mobility as it did with Memnon at the Granicus; he was effectively penned in by the Gulf of Issus on his right flank, the river in front of him, and the narrow strip of land before the mountains on his left flank. On the opposite side of the river, Alexander could spread out his own troops, and he took full advantage of this: he stretched his right wing much further out than the left wing of his enemy.

Lysander explained to me later that Alexander had also noticed that where the riverbanks were less steep, the Persians had fenced them with palisades. This made it clear that they would not advance to the fight and would probably shrink from man-to-man combat, relying instead on their cavalry and archers. This was all Alexander needed. Positioning himself – unusually, on foot – at the head of his guard infantry, he led them swiftly across the streambed into the enemy ranks. And this time, he carefully chose to attack the Persian rather than the Greek mercenary infantry.

I learned afterwards from Erebos and his Krypteian spies that Darius had further stacked the cards against himself well before the battle. He had ignored the advice of Charidamus, one of his trusted Greek generals, who had advised Darius to divide his forces and allow him (Charidamus) to fight alone against Alexander. Darius dismissed these words of wisdom; he could not possibly lose to this young Macedonian upstart. Annoyed at being ignored, Charidamus unfortunately made a few ill-chosen comments in Greek about Persians. Which Darius perfectly understood and, offended, immediately had one of his most capable generals executed.

From our position on Alexander's strong right flank, firing across the water in shock-and-awe charges as we did at the Granicus, we could see the battle going badly from the start for Darius. Unable to manoeuvre as they would have liked, he and his men were soon on the defensive. Alexander, on the other hand, was able to use his mighty phalanx formation. His right flank extended to the mountains, and his left to the sea. He had three battalions on the right and four to the left, with heavy infantry in the middle. Despite all the Persians' efforts, their attempts to drive us back across the river failed.

Having mowed down Darius' left flank, Alexander and his Companion Cavalry turned towards the Persian centre – where he spotted Darius. Darius' brother, Oxyathres, attempted to block Alexander's charge but failed. Darius fled the battle, at first in his chariot; this soon got bogged down, so he continued his flight on horseback. Alexander had sustained a serious thigh wound but pursued Darius until nightfall. At that point, he had to return, because he had departed the battle with his left flank, under the leadership of his chief general, Parmenio, under heavy pressure from Darius' right flank.

But he need not have worried. When the Persians saw their leader flee, their resistance collapsed; now they were dying, not from Macedonian iron but from being trampled in the retreat. There were many deaths and casualties in the battle of Issus; Darius lost about twenty thousand men and we lost around seven thousand. For many days afterwards, the burying of the dead and the tending of the injured went on.

*

Once again, my Myrmidons are playing a large part in helping the medics, with their bandages and cheerful words. And rumours are going round about all the plunder that has been found in the Persian camp. Penelope tells me about the king's tent. 'Amazing, boss! Full of splendid furniture, and gold this and silver that.' She giggles. 'The Big A went off to bathe in Darius' bath, saying,' she intones pompously, '"Let us now cleanse ourselves from the toils of war in the bath of Darius!"'

I'm sitting eating with Lysander as she reports. He says, 'And there was more than gold and silver, wasn't there, Penelope?'

She nods. 'It seems that the Persian king likes to take his family to war with him; his wife and two daughters, and even his mother, poor old thing!'

Lysander explains, 'Alexander has promised them that they will be safe. He has told them that Darius is not dead, and that they need not fear any harm from him, Alexander, as he seeks only dominion, not blood. He has assured them that they will be provided with everything that they had been used to receive from Darius.'

I comment, 'So he sees himself as stepping into Darius' shoes, does he?'

Penelope laughs. 'Well, he's already got into his bath!'

Lysander replies, in a quiet voice that reminds me of his father, 'Alexander has won almost half the Persian empire, after eighteen months' campaigning at no great distance from base. It's a remarkable achievement.'

In a fit of realism, Darius later declared himself willing to legitimise Alexander's conquest; the conditions were that his mother, wife, and children must be returned, and Alexander must promise to campaign no further. His offer was rejected with scorn, with Alexander replying that there could never be two suns. The following missive was taken to Darius: '*In future, send to me as the King of Asia and tell me of your needs addressing me not as an equal but as master of all your possessions. Otherwise, I will deal with you as a miscreant. If you challenge for the Kingship, stand and fight, and do not run away, since I shall go wherever you are.*'

*

It was to be a long while before Alexander went where Darius was. First, he had to campaign in Egypt. Long regarded as the jewel in Persia's crown, Egypt was a satrapy of the Persian empire, which was critical to Alexander's goals. He also had very personal reasons for pursuing this campaign, which were to do with how he saw himself; namely, as a demi-god with a mission.

So with Issus sorted, we find ourselves on the march southwards into Phoenicia, which is Egypt's neighbour. The first two cities on our route, Byblos and Sidon, capitulate without any bloodshed. It's very different with the mighty island city of Tyre. Alexander has sent ahead a request to sacrifice to Heracles in Tyre. On the way there, he's met by envoys from Tyre, who tell him that he's welcome to sacrifice in Old Tyre, which is on the mainland. They can hardly have been surprised when Alexander insisted on carrying out the ritual inside the heavily fortified new city. His was hardly a subtle stratagem. Naturally, the Tyrians refused. As far as Alexander is concerned, this is tantamount to a declaration of war.

So that night, we're camped not far from Tyre, and Alexander convenes a council of war with his generals. Lysander told me afterwards that our leader explained the vital importance of securing all Phoenician cities before advancing on Egypt. Tyre was a stronghold for the Persian fleet and could not be left behind untouched to threaten our rear. It was agreed that a last-ditch attempt would be made to prevent a long siege, so heralds are sent to Tyre, demanding that the city surrender. In a move reminiscent of Athens' and Sparta's treatment of Persian envoys some time ago, the Macedonian ambassadors are executed, and their bodies hurled into the sea.

The Tyrians had every reason to be confident of withstanding a siege. Their city lay around half a mile offshore; the walls facing the landward side towered at least as high as the mighty walls of Babylon that my father told me about. They had a powerful navy and a mercenary army, and they had withstood many mighty sieges in the past. So they began their preparations and evacuated most of the women and children to their colony at Carthage, leaving behind some forty thousand defenders. Apparently, Carthage also promised to send ships and soldiers.

Alexander launched his attack, firstly, by occupying Old Tyre, which was undefended. Then, he turned his infantry into engineers and began to construct a causeway across the channel, towards the walls of the island city. There was plenty of material available from the rocks, timbers, and rubble taken from the buildings of the old city. At first, the work went well, because the water near the mainland was shallow. It began to get a whole lot trickier the nearer they got to the citadel; the seafloor near the city shelved sharply, to a depth of eighteen feet. To make things trickier still, there was now missile fire from the city walls.

With two bloody seaport sieges already under his belt, Alexander was undeterred. He had his engineers build two siege towers from timber covered with rawhide and positioned them at the end of the causeway. Artillery engines at the top of these towers began to return fire at the walls; to give additional protection, the work gangs erected timber palisades. Work got underway again, and Alexander spent a lot of time on the causeway, giving small gifts of money to his sweating labourers. Lysander and I agreed that this habit of leading by personal example was among the young king's finest qualities.

However, the Tyrians' iron resolve to fight back soon showed itself. They took an old horse transport ship and filled it with combustible material: chaff, torches, pitch, and sulphur. They slung double yard-arms out at right angles to the mast and hooked up cauldrons brimming with a volatile, inflammable oil. The stern of the ship was ballasted to lift the bows clear of the water, then two galleys towed this lethal fireship to the end of the causeway and drove all three ships aground. Lighting the materials aboard the vessel from Hades, the crew all managed to swim to safety. And horrors broke loose on the causeway. The two towers ignited, siege engines burned, and the protective palisades were destroyed. The fires were followed up by hosts of Tyrians in small boats landing on the causeway, attacking the besiegers as they attempted to douse the flames.

This deathly and demoralising fightback deterred Alexander not in the least. We had to admire his resolve, in ordering the causeway to be widened and more towers to be built. But he also switched his strategy, realising that naval superiority was the key to taking Tyre. He set off on a ship round-up, to friendly ports in and around the Mediterranean: Sidon, Byblos, Aradus, Rhodes, Lycia, Cilicia, and his native Macedon. The kings of Cyprus also sent another 120 ships to Sidon, bringing Alexander's total to around 220 vessels. His manpower had also been substantially increased, with one of his commanders, Cleander, arriving leading four thousand mercenaries recruited from Greece.

So you can imagine the shock and dismay of the observers on the city walls of Tyre, when this vast fleet suddenly fills the horizon. The Tyrians were now the outnumbered ones, which must have made a pleasant change for Alexander. Oh, and the Carthaginians had suffered a slight memory loss: 'Help? What help did we promise?' So Tyre was now isolated.

The size of our fleet made a naval engagement out of the question; the best the Tyrians could do was blockade the entrances to their two harbours. They floated a boom across the mouth of the southern harbour and moored triremes in line across the entrance of the northern one. Alexander tested the strength of these counter-measures with an assault on the northern harbour, where three Tyrian galleys were rammed head-on and sunk. But he contented himself for now with arranging his fleet to, effectively, blockade the blockades. More siege engines were mounted on the causeway and on anchored ships, and he began a sustained bombardment of the city.

The big problem here was that Alexander couldn't get his ships close to the city, because the Tyrians had hurled massive rocks into the sea beneath the walls. I can guess what you're thinking now, and you're right. Mountains of giant boulders were not going to bother Alexander. His ships lassoed the beasts and towed them away from the walls. The Tyrians responded by cladding some of their ships in armour plating and sallying forth to cut the anchor cables of the besieging ships. Alexander batted back by armouring some of his own vessels and using them as a screen in front of his siege ships. So the Tyrians used divers to cut the cables. Alexander's was the final blow in this extraordinary naval tit-for-tat; he replaced the rope cables

'I SHALL GO WHEREVER YOU ARE'

with chains. More boulders were lassoed from the causeway and hauled out of the water with cranes.

The besieged were now resorting to the cruellest of measures. And you might want to skip this bit, too, as it tears me apart with horror and pity. Throughout the sea battles, the defenders had been pouring cauldrons of red-hot sand over the walls onto the besieging ships. This was a truly terrible weapon; carried by the wind, it set vessels alight and penetrated clothing and armour, reducing the poor men on the receiving end to charred, blistered agony.

In a desperate bid to counter-attack at sea, the Tyrians spread concealing sails across the mouth of the northern harbour and prepared to do battle. Thirteen galleys were manned with their finest oarsmen and marines, and in the heat of a Mediterranean afternoon, they silently rowed out of the northern harbour in a single line. They had picked their line of attack well, as most of Alexander's ships blockading them at this harbour were under-manned. It was a surprise attack, and a ferocious one; Alexander lost two ships and many more were scattered.

In typical style, Alexander personally led the fightback, with five triremes and as many quinqueremes as he could muster. Sailing around the island, he pounced on the Tyrian flotilla, which promptly scattered and fled for home. Two of their galleys were captured, and more were damaged; at least, unlike the Persians, the Tyrians knew how to swim, and most managed to get ashore to safety.

By now, Alexander's patience was running out. With the boulders removed, he brought his ships directly beneath the walls and pounded them with battering rams. At first, this had limited success, although a small breach was made in the southern wall.

He waited for three days before resuming his assault, this time with diversionary attacks occupying the defenders' attention. While the Tyrians were looking the other way, two of Alexander's ships with bridging equipment approached the breach that had been made in the southern wall. On board these ships were Alexander himself, a number of hand-picked officers, and the crème de la crème of his elite shield-carriers and spearmen. This time, the Macedonians managed to force their way onto the wall. Admetus, commander of the shield-carriers, was the first man onto the battlements and was sadly killed by a spear as he urged his men onward.

But the assault succeeded, and soon our army was pouring down into the city itself; more were entering from the harbours. The surviving Tyrians retreated to the Agenorium, an old fortress in the northern part of the city, but they held out only for a brief period. And I'm sorry to say that, after a long and bitter siege, our men were not inclined to be merciful. For months, they had endured grinding labour, while being tormented by artillery, archery, and missiles; and they had witnessed the slaughter of their captured comrades on the city walls. Skip the next bit if you can't bear to read about the bloodier facts of battle. Six thousand Tyrians were killed when the city was taken, and a further two thousand were crucified on the beach. Thirty thousand were sold into slavery. Among those spared were the king and his family, and a number of Carthaginian pilgrims who took sanctuary in the temple of Melqart. Our own losses were in the hundreds rather than thousands, after seven months which had tested our army's endurance and fortitude to the limit.

And so, Alexander finally made his sacrifice to Heracles, and held a torch race and triumphal procession through the streets of the city. I wasn't part of that, and neither was Lysander. He had been on Alexander's ship that breached the walls, one of the king's hand-picked officers. When Admetus fell, Lysander took his place in urging on the men and received a vicious spear wound in his left shoulder: damage which he only admitted to when Alexander saw him on the point of passing out from blood loss and called for his medics.

I'm changing Lysander's blood-soaked bandages in one of the houses that have been commandeered for the wounded when he slowly opens his eyes. I lift his head and hold a flask of water to his lips; he drinks. Then, he murmurs, 'Stupid of me.'

'No, smart. One, it's not your sword arm. Two, I've still got plenty of the yarrow you collected for me.'

Despite the pain he's in, that spark of mischief is back in his eyes. 'You're sure you wouldn't like me to search for reinforcements, my lady?'

Suddenly, there are voices at the door, and the blaze of a torch dims the candlelight. Alexander's powerful figure fills the doorway, his bodyguards behind him. He comes in and stands beside Lysander, as I put a final, tight knot in the new bandage.

He says to me, 'Has he lost much blood?'

I stand respectfully. 'The flow has stopped now, sir. But he has lost a great deal.'

He glances at the bloody bandages on the floor, then looks at Lysander. 'Your bravery in taking the place of Admetus at the head of the charge will be decorated, Commander.'

Lysander has struggled to raise himself out of respect, propped up on his good arm. 'He will be sorely missed, sir.'

'He will receive posthumous honours, and his widow and children will be cared for by the state, as is the custom.' Alexander looks back at me. 'See to it that he gets plenty of rest. You and your Myrmidons are doing fine work, supporting our medics.' As swiftly as he arrived, he and his men are gone.

Exhausted, Lysander lies back down. I reach for the water and support his head while I hold the flask to his lips. He drinks again. 'Can I get you some food?'

He smiles, shaking his head slowly, the mischief sparkling again now that we are alone. His good arm goes round me and draws me gently to him. Our second kiss lasts considerably longer than the first.

SIX

'SQUABBLING CHILDREN WHO COULD THROW THUNDERBOLTS!'

Once Lysander starts to regain his strength, we go for quiet walks outside the city walls. Along the beaches, the burned siege engines are being repaired where possible, ready for the next assault. Lysander has been privy to Alexander's meetings with his generals, where Persian warships were top of the agenda. 'Alexander is convinced – and we all agree with him – that he cannot successfully attack Darius until he has completely destroyed Persian naval power in the Mediterranean. His words to General Parmenio, over a year ago, were "to conquer the Persian fleet from the land".'

'And that's what he's begun with Tyre?'

'The Persian navy, their army, and their seaports are interdependent; the vulnerable hinge is the seaport itself, which is why they are so heavily fortified. Tyre was the strongest port in the Eastern Mediterranean.'

'And Gaza is next on the way to Egypt…'

'The fortress is located at the edge of a desert and overlooks the main route to Egypt.'

'Who is in charge?'

'Batis – a eunuch and, Erebos tells me, a very proud, brave, and loyal man. He expects to hold Egypt in subjection until Darius can raise another army and confront Alexander from Gaza.'

'But Alexander wants to pre-empt that.'

'If he can bring down Gaza, he will have wiped out the Persian presence in the Mediterranean.'

'I expect that Batis is going to be ready for him!'

'He will know of the fall of Tyre and will have provisioned himself for a long siege.'

*

The fortress is positioned on the main road that goes from Persian Assyria to Egypt. Its commanding position, overlooking the surrounding area, makes it easy to dominate what is a hotbed of dissent. The walls encircle the citadel, and they are colossal; they must be sixty feet high. Alexander decides that the southern walls are the weakest; so the backbreaking work begins, of constructing three large earthwork platforms abutting those huge walls, from which to fire on the defenders. He's brought towers and catapults with him, and we're expecting the arrival of the repaired siege engines from Tyre in a few days' time.

As soon as he sees what's happening, Batis launches a hail of missiles from the walls, and hordes of mounted archers and spearmen assault the troops labouring on the earthworks. We're expecting this; the Myrmidons go into all-out shock-and-awe charges, downing swathes of attackers. Following hot on our heels, the cavalry mounts a headlong assault. But the Gazans fight back hard; it's only when Alexander turns up with his elite troops, Lysander and his cohort among them, that the defenders are forced to retreat. Alexander takes a hit in the shoulder from a projectile that would have slain two standard soldiers; it makes a dent in his shield and his armour but doesn't even unseat him.

Shortly after this skirmish, the siege engines arrive by ship from Tyre, and the battering of the walls begins in earnest. With the force of attack from the catapults, large sections of the walls are broken. Alexander also deploys sappers to tunnel beneath the fortifications and undermine the walls. But the first three attempts to enter the city all fail, such is the bitter determination and endurance of the Gazans.

At one point, they try deception. An Arab mercenary comes out waving a surrender flag; he gets into Alexander's presence and goes for him with a knife, actually managing to inflict a wound before he's struck down by the bodyguards. This inflames Alexander, and, I think, is the cause of the atrocities that follow. You may now wish to skip right to the end of the Gaza story, but, in justice to the victims, it has to be told.

The fourth attempt sees our army entering the city. The males are put to the sword, all ten thousand of them. The lives of women and children are spared, but they are all sold into slavery. But now comes the worst example of Alexander's cruelty that Lysander and I saw during the whole time that we campaigned with him. Worse still, because Alexander generally admires courage in an enemy.

Batis is brought before his conqueror and proudly refuses to kneel or even speak to him, despite all Alexander's threats. Enraged, Alexander says, 'You shall not have the death you wanted. Instead, you can expect to suffer whatever torment can be devised against a prisoner.'

So he decides to follow the example of his hero, Achilles, after he killed Hector, and dishonoured his body by dragging it from a chariot around the walls of Troy. Except that Alexander does this to Batis while he is still alive. That doesn't make what Achilles did any better; instead, it makes Alexander's cruelty an order of magnitude worse.

If this sickens and angers you so much, you can hardly speak, it does that to me, too. I have to quit this horrible scene and go down to the sea to get some air, away from the stench of brutality and murder. Lysander finds me, and we walk. For a long time, neither of us utters a word. Then, I remember something my father told me. Turning to Lysander, I say, 'Can we sit on these rocks for a while? I think my namesake has something to say to us.'

Lysander knows about the Athenian Lydia, because my father told the twins about her at around the same time he told me, when I was aged seven and they would have been eight. So he knows how gifted she was, and how tragically

'SQUABBLING CHILDREN'

young she died. But he doesn't know what she thought about the gods, and I think that now is the time to reflect on her thoughts.

As we gaze out across the Mediterranean in the dimming light of evening, I begin. 'My father was reading from the *Iliad* to his little pupil one morning when she showed him what a wise head she had on such young shoulders. They were at the bit where Achilles is sulking in his tent because Briseis, his beloved slave girl, has been taken from him by Agamemnon. My father suggested to Lydia that, perhaps, Achilles was sulking with good reason. And she replied that, perhaps he was, but because he was staying out of the fighting, men were being needlessly killed. She said to my father, that she thought this was Achilles' chance to show he was above Agamemnon's egoism.'

Lysander murmurs, 'Wise head on young shoulders, indeed. Go on.'

'My father agreed that, if Achilles had only decided to fight at that time, the Trojan War could have taken a very different turn. And Lydia said that it was up to the mortals to set an example to the gods, who had started the war in the first place. She described the gods as "no better than squabbling children who could throw thunderbolts!". And here we have Alexander, paying such reverence to squabbling children!'

Lysander says thoughtfully, 'And behaving like a murderous, squabbling child himself. As I did, once.'

I put a hand on his cheek and gently turn his face to me. 'I don't believe that you would ever have harmed your brother!'

I can see tears in Lysander's eyes as he looks at me. 'Thank you, my lady.'

*

There can be no doubt that Egypt meant something uniquely special to Alexander. It was here that his reverence to local Egyptian gods would win the acclaim of the people of Egypt. Paradoxically, it was also here that he would seek to confirm his own divinity; logical to consider himself a god, perhaps, in view of his completely undefeated battle history.

Lysander and I think that it was Alexander's acute sense of his own mortality that drove him relentlessly to seek deification. He was very like his hero, Achilles. The son of a goddess, but a mortal father, Achilles grew up with the knowledge that he was 'doomed to live but for a little season', not forever, like his mother; he was aware that he had little time to cover himself in glory before he died. He did the opposite, when he dishonoured the remains of the dead Hector. No Spartan would have done that to a fallen foe.

Alexander was even more like Achilles than he probably thought he was; because it was an act of monumental horror to kill Batis in the way he did. The only hero in sight, martyred for his own courage, was the proud and magnificent Persian. Despite being a eunuch, Batis was undisputedly the alpha male of the two. The man who had him killed in that way was behaving like a cowardly despot.

So it sticks in my gullet when Alexander is given a hero's welcome as we arrive in Egypt, at Pelusium; the navy follows

'SQUABBLING CHILDREN'

shortly afterwards. The Persians have been ruling Egypt since conquering the kingdom ten years ago. The Persian currently in charge – the satrap, or governor – is called Mazaces. Seeing the huge crowd of Egyptians greeting Alexander and his army as their liberators, having heard of Darius' flight at Issus and the fall of Gaza, and with no soldiers to challenge the invaders, Mazaces wisely decides to join in the welcome.

Leaving the army to rest at Pelusium, Alexander now orders Lysander and his cohort, and me and the Myrmidons, to come with him to Memphis. Situated on the Nile, this city has been the traditional seat of power for Egyptian rulers over centuries. Lysander and I exchange glances; we know we're up for yet another show to which the Big A, as Penelope calls him, wants us to bear witness.

And it literally is a show, with athletic and musical contests, attended by the most celebrated athletes and artists, who have come all the way from Greece. But these are sideshows compared with Alexander's visit to sacrifice to the Apis bull, at the temple. The cult of the Apis bull is especially strong at Memphis. The temple itself is an imposing, palatial building of soaring height, with flight upon flight of marble steps, richly inlaid with historic and mythical imagery, leading up to the priests who guard the earthly incarnation of Apis, the sacred bull itself.

This is the only Egyptian deity to which Alexander sacrifices during his visit. Lysander, who has read his history, explains why, in low tones, as we look on with our troops, and salute at the correct times: 'The Persian Empire has invaded Egypt twice in the past few hundred years: the

Persian king Cambyses, and King Artaxerxes the Third. On both occasions, the Persian kings showed complete contempt for the Apis bull deity when they reached Memphis. They actually committed the sacrilege of having the sacred bull slain! It was a gross sign of Persian contempt for Egyptian religious belief.'

I'm beginning to get it. 'So, by sacrificing to the Apis bull, Alexander is portraying himself as the opposite of the Persian invaders?'

Lysander nods. 'Exactly. Here is Alexander, in an act of deference to the Egyptian religion that completely sets him apart from the Persian invaders.'

I watch as Alexander carries out the ritual sacrifice to the sacred Apis bull, kneeling in all humility. 'And here is Alexander, the king who has liberated the Egyptians from Persian rule. He respects and honours local gods, while leaving room for his own.'

Lysander turns to me, his blue eyes intense. 'Can you wonder that he is being proclaimed the new pharaoh? It's a political masterstroke.'

*

Alexander's next act in his Greek drama was to found the jewel of the Mediterranean, Alexandria. He named many cities after himself, but the Egyptian Alexandria is by far the most illustrious. Many say that the city is perhaps the greatest achievement of Alexander's military campaigns; I agree with them because, instead of destruction, he was, on this rare occasion, involved in creation. Alexander

'SQUABBLING CHILDREN'

intended the new city to be a Greek colony, where he could leave his veterans and the wounded to start a new life; I can guess what they thought of this when they must have been longing for home. But it was to become far more than that, including a major trade route to the Aegean sea.

Alexander played a leading role in the design of the general layout, indicating where the agora – or marketplace – should go, the number of temples, and the precise limits of the outer defences. Among the temples were one to Poseidon and a second to Hephaestos, the Greek god of fire and metallurgy, which would interest my armourer father.

In designing his city, Alexander took advice from the best architects and he also – according to his account – followed his dreams. Apparently, he chanced one night in his sleep to see a grey-haired old man appearing to stand by him and pronounce these verses:

An island lies, where loud the billows roar,
Pharos, they call it, on the Egyptian shore.

At that time, Pharos was an island above a mouth of the River Nile, although it has since been joined to the mainland by a causeway. Alexander hastened to Pharos, and was delighted by the location, on a long neck of land, stretching like an isthmus between large lagoons and shallow waters on one side, and the sea on the other, creating a spacious harbour. I have never had a rhyming dream; probably because I can't write poetry.

And now comes another story, which does have a ring of truth about it. Apparently, they had no chalk to draw out the lines of the city in the black soil. So Alexander and his architects laid out the lines by scattering flour, creating a semi-circular shape and drawing equal straight lines to the centre, rather like a cloak. Alexander was congratulating himself on the overall look when a large flock of birds rose in a black cloud from the river and the lagoons, and devoured every morsel of flour, completely obliterating the lines.

Even Alexander was a bit bothered by this omen, but the augurs came to the rescue; they said it was a sign that the city he was about to build would not only 'abound in all things within itself, but also be the nurse and feeder of many nations'. This breathtaking transformation, from portent of doom into glory, far surpassed any pronouncements made by Alexander during the course of his campaigns. Satisfied, he told the workmen to get on with it while he went to visit the oracle at the temple of Ammon, to pursue the burning question.

*

He wished Lysander and me to accompany him, without our cohorts, on this mission. And I was very grateful that we only had the four of us – Hephaestion came too – to look after, because this three hundred-mile trek across the Sahara desert nearly cost us our lives. What saved our lives was my black Arabian's ability to seek out water. Like his sire, Arion, Pegasus could scent water from many miles away. I have no doubt that, without him, we would have perished. It is a sign of Alexander's almost fanatical passion for pursuing the question of his own divinity that he approached this trek as a personal quest, not as he would have done a battle that he had to win. Forget planning – there was none.

The temple of Ammon, where the oracle resides, is at Siwa Oasis. Good news, I hear you say – oasis means water. While Alexander went in to consult the oracle, Lysander and I filled every container we had, and the horses drank long and deep.

Apparently, the regional god Ammon was the local manifestation of Zeus, from whom Alexander believed he was descended (from which family tree, I have no idea, as his father was definitely Philip of Macedon and his mother Olympias, one of Philip's many wives). What we do know, via Hephaestion, is that Alexander was greeted by the oracle as the son of Ammon, the Egyptian god, and he was given favourable omens for completing his invasion of Persia. Our king then consulted the oracle alone, in the central sanctuary, and asked if he was the son of Zeus. He emerged looking satisfied. But he never shared the words of the oracle with anyone. Possibly, because even the Alexander PR machine would have had problems with this one. I mean, how many fathers can you have?

On the ride back to Memphis, through the blazing desert, Lysander and I discuss this. He says, 'I think that Alexander wants to appear to be an Egyptian deity in Egypt, a Persian deity in Persia, and, as the monarch in the Macedonian tradition, the chief intermediary between his people and the gods back at home.'

'He just has to remember where he is at any one time.'

'Especially in Macedon – he knows that no Greek would ever bend the knee to worship a mortal!'

'So now it's business as usual, is it?'

'We begin the march against Darius as soon as we get back to Memphis.'

*

Alexander thought that he would give battle to Darius at Babylon, the traditional seat of power for the King of Kings. But when he learned of the Persian king's presence at Gaugamela, a place several hundred miles northwards of Babylon, he changed plans. For Alexander, it was all to gain at Gaugamela – Babylon, Persepolis, and Susa would all be his. The largest part of the Persian empire at his command. And, Lysander and I would remind ourselves, maybe then we could finally go home, with our loyal troops, having fulfilled our commitments. At least, that's what we hoped.

Lysander and I were informed en route by Erebos that Darius had put together quite a different army from the Issus encounter. He had brought fighters from as far away as India; estimates of his army varied widely but included fifteen elephants (on the day, there wasn't an elephant in sight, which was a relief; horses are, understandably, freaked out by elephants, and have to be specially trained to deal with them). Darius also had two hundred scythed chariots, which on the right ground can deal out serious injury. He was using longer swords and lances, and his cavalry too had grown. According to Erebos, Darius also seemed to have learned lessons from the Granicus and Issus. The terrain of Gaugamela was much wider, so he could make use of his chariots and deploy his cavalry far more effectively, which

'SQUABBLING CHILDREN'

had been impossible at Issus. He prepared the ground as a killing field, clearing the ground for his own troops, and placing obstacles and traps to impede the advance of Alexander's forces. It must have seemed to the Persian king that, for once, the odds were stacked in his favour.

Our army, some forty thousand infantry and seven thousand cavalry (once again, heavily outnumbered by Darius), made camp around five miles from the foe. Then, Alexander assembled a small scouting party and looked down from a hill, unobserved, at the Persian preparations. As luck would have it, he also came upon an advance party sent out by Darius. While some fled, several were captured and told of Darius' numbers, and the traps and obstacles he had prepared.

The night before the battle, Alexander held a council of his generals; Lysander, now among the elite officers, was there and told me later what had happened. Parmenio, the commander of Alexander's left flank, and cautious because of his age and experience, suggested that the large size of Darius' forces called for us to attack at night. However, Alexander disagreed. He said it would mean stealing a victory and give Darius an excuse for losing to him. Later, as he addressed his men, he spoke of the coming battle and reassured his superstitious Macedonian troops that an earlier eclipse of the moon was a sign of victory. Then, he made sure that his men were well fed and well rested. Darius' men, of course, stayed awake all night, waiting for an attack that never came.

On the day of the battle, Alexander apparently overslept, providing still more reassurance of his confidence in a Macedonian victory. (I don't think he overslept – he just said he did, as part of his well-oiled PR machinery, to show how relaxed he was about winning. Still, if it works, don't knock it.) With troops having taken up battle stations, Alexander looked across the battlefield towards the legions of Persians and called out individual Macedonian soldiers by name, speaking of their bravery in other battles and asking them to fight once again for Macedon. And frankly, with their young king naming them personally, in front of the whole army, who would not have followed him to the ends of the earth and fought like a lion for him?

The finishing touch was when an eagle – a favourite creature of Zeus – flew overhead and towards Darius. Even Alexander could not have orchestrated this powerful omen of victory. And you had to hand it to him – he had prepared for this fight well, his razor-sharp brain omitting neither the smallest detail nor the remotest possibility.

So, picture it. As usual, Alexander and his Companion Cavalry took up position on the right flank, while General Parmenio held the left flank. In the middle, like a wall of iron, was the highly trained Macedonian phalanx, with more light infantry and archers on either side. As usual, too, we Myrmidons were stationed to provide the cutting edge for the Companion Cavalry on the right flank. But Alexander also did something different; he placed infantry at angles on the ends of both the right and left flanks, in case of a possible flanking manoeuvre by the Persians (who, you will remember, now had more space than in either of the two preceding battles). And he placed additional Greek

'SQUABBLING CHILDREN'

infantry to the rear of the centre, where the phalanx was; you'll see why shortly.

As the battle began, Alexander carried out an ingenious feint, which completely fooled the enemy. He and his Companion Cavalry, with my mounted archers storming ahead of them, arrows flying, moved to their right at an oblique angle. Following Darius' orders, the Persians, under their general Bessus, moved to their left in an attempt to outflank Alexander. As the Persians moved further and further to their left, and into terrain that had not been cleared, this created a gap in their line. Seeing the opening, Alexander formed his men into a wedge and quickly moved to his left and into the gap, charging Darius, who was by now in a state of shock. This was a tactic pioneered by Xenophon, who would often make it appear as if his army was going to fight along many fronts, leading the enemy to space their troops so sparsely that he could blast through their thinned ranks with ease. In fact, Xenophon introduced the whole concept of the feint: part of his ingenious use of deceit, to win battles using his head as much as his sword.

While Alexander was challenging the Persians on the right, Darius' scythed chariots galloped towards the Macedonian centre, where the mighty phalanx awaited them. This did not have the effect that Darius had been hoping for. As the chariots approached, the phalanx deftly opened ranks, allowing the deadly armed wheels to simply pass through. This is a manoeuvre that looks far easier than it actually is, but the Macedonian infantry were probably the most highly trained and experienced in the world. As the scythed chariots shot through the opened ranks, without doing any harm at all, the infantry that Alexander had stationed behind the phalanx were waiting for them and set on them with flying spears followed by hand-to-hand combat, which Persians try to avoid, and Greeks love.

Back on the right, Alexander had spotted Darius and launched a spear at the stunned king, missing him by inches. As far as Darius was concerned, this was Issus all over again. He fled, the same way as before: at first in his chariot and then on horseback. Seeing him go, his army scattered. And it was all over, bar the burying of the dead and the patching-up of the living.

The performance of Macedon's superb phalanx, in being so swift to react and open up, and then close and tighten ranks again, was one of the finest spectacles I witnessed in the whole time I campaigned with Alexander. And I hugely admire his battle savvy: how he reconnoitred the ground, learned from his scouts and from captured advance forces, and how he planned ahead to create a gap in the advancing front line so that he could fool the enemy, and strike hard where it hurt. This was Alexander's supreme moment as a leader. He should be remembered for his greatness as a commander from Gaugamela. It had none of the sordid butchery of previous battles and sieges. It had everything of penetrating insight and getting inside the mind of the enemy. I will always salute him as the best of leaders for what he did at Gaugamela; Lysander feels the same way.

The consequences of the battle of Gaugamela were far-reaching. The great Persian army no longer existed to protect Babylonia, the wealthiest satrapy of the empire, or its capital, Babylon, one of the largest cities in the world.

'SQUABBLING CHILDREN'

The population of Babylon had no means to resist our army. Alexander's campaign was succeeding splendidly, but his crusade was far from over.

The usual looting of the Persian camp took place before we advanced south towards the city whose name means 'Gate of the Gods'. At a place called Sippar, the Persian commander, Mazaeus, formally surrendered Babylon to Alexander. We entered the city via the blue-tiled, sixty-foot-high Ishtar Gate, through which my father went as an envoy for Athens, and over which he and Uncle Leon and their early strike force shot flaming arrows not long after.

Glancing back to where I can just pick out Lysander riding at the head of his men, I remember that Ishtar is the Persian goddess of both love and war.

As we move up Procession Street, our victorious king is riding in the Persian royal chariot, not on his beloved warhorse, Bucephalus. It's a sign of things to come.

SEVEN

GATE OF THE GODS

The Babylonians recognised the new ruler as 'King of the world', which is close to the Greek title that Alexander adopted after the battle of Issus – 'King of Asia'. And now that Alexander had become ruler, rule was what he had to do. Firstly, he promised that the buildings of Babylon would be protected, and the citizens of Babylon safe. He appointed the Persian commander, Mazaeus, as satrap (governor) of Babylonia. Alexander had appointed another Persian commander, Doloaspis, in Egypt. Lysander and I understood, as did his officers, that this was a military necessity; satraps will come to terms, and be loyal, far sooner if they know they will be re-appointed. Not everyone saw it that way.

We were five weeks in the capital of Babylonia before marching again, in November. Reinforcements had arrived, and everything was ready for the final attack on the four major cities of the Persian empire: Susa, Persepolis, Pasargadae, and Ecbatana. During the march, Alexander appointed several new officers. Up to that point, the Macedonian military units had corresponded to provinces of the Macedonian kingdom and had been commanded by local chiefs; so, for example, a Thessalian aristocrat commanded the Thessalian cavalry. Now, the officers were selected by merit. Lysander commented to me, 'Interesting. He does not want to perpetuate the regional divisions in Macedon.'

We were riding together in the heat of the day, with a long cloud of dust rising from the marching columns.

'But will the men be as loyal to an officer who is not one of them?'

'His father did a great deal to turn the Macedonian army into a unified, professional fighting force. I think Alexander sees this as the logical next step away from tribalism.'

'What do you think?'

He gazes ahead at the heat shimmer on the horizon as he weighs up his answer. 'I think he is relying on the force of his personality to command loyalty to him over all else as their leader.'

We reached Susa in December. The garrison commander, a Persian named Abulites, surrendered the town and its treasures, and was immediately re-appointed as satrap of this region called Susiana.

And here happened another of those events which Alexander is so clever at turning to his advantage. He took his place on the throne in the apadana (throne hall) and found that the seat was too high for his feet to reach the small, built-in bench of the throne; he was not that tall, as I observed when I first met him, although of a very muscular build. One of his courtiers brought a little table, which was just the right height. Now, before anyone could read into this less-than-favourable omen, that Alexander was not tall enough to sit on the throne of his predecessor, he himself put it about that his feet had been on Darius' table. This sent Penelope into fits of laughter, as being simply another bath episode. And I have to say that the significance of the feet of the Big A, as she called him, on Darius' table was completely lost on me. Lysander neatly by-passed it with one of his sunny smiles.

After re-organising Susiana, Alexander left behind one thousand veterans, and we marched on towards the heartland of the Persian empire. Here, we were entering hostile and difficult terrain, where we could not claim to be liberating the inhabitants. The passes of the Zagros mountains, between Susiana and the Persian homeland, were fiercely guarded, and we knew there would be heavy losses on our part. So, to spread the risk, Alexander divided his troops. His trusted general Parmenio was to take a southerly route around the mountains, while Alexander would take the main road and force the Persian Gate.

The satrap of Persis, the formidably fierce Ariobarzanes, occupied the pass. And for once, we Myrmidons were powerless to help, when arrows were raining down on us from above. So I got permission from Alexander to let us try a sortie around the pass, to see if we could find a mountain path to outflank the Persians, like they did to the Spartans' legendary Leonidas at Thermopylae. It was a local man who betrayed Leonidas and his courageous few, but we didn't need the help of a traitor. The Myrmidons quickly found a path to the Persians' rear and reported it to Alexander. He waited until dark, then a cohort of heavily armed infantry climbed up the cliff via the path and stormed the Persian Gate stronghold.

The look on the faces of the Persian garrison in the mountain must have been shock personified. Because of our heavy losses, Alexander was not inclined to be kind; and, for once, Lysander and I understood. The Persians should have known that surrender was the best option, after the civilised way that Alexander had treated Babylon and Susa.

The look on Alexander's face afterwards, as he came round to personally congratulate us, was interesting, too. It reminded me of his intense gaze after we thrashed the opposition in the mounted relay at the Games. 'You have, Myrmidons, the ability to keep surprising me.'

I return, 'As long as that helps you to keep surprising the Persians, sir.' His eyes rest on me with that same look for a tiny second more, before he moves on. But not before Lysander's blue eyes have taken it all in.

*

As a result of our victory at the Persian Gate, in the following January, our army stood in Persepolis, the capital of the Persian empire. Many inhabitants fled, and I'm sad to say that some committed suicide, but the governor surrendered the city and its treasure. And now, Alexander did what generals have to do to keep the loyalty of their armies: he gave the city to his soldiers. They had seen the riches of the East on a number of occasions but had never so far been offered their share. So, the city was looted; the only exception being the royal palace. I don't wish to be disingenuous here, having disapproved of looting the enemy camp in the past. But let's face it, these soldiers had followed Alexander with such unfailing loyalty, helped him to win his many battles and sieges for so long, that their steadfastness deserved rewarding.

Almost at the same time, with Alexander having split his army, General Parmenio captured nearby Pasargadae. This was Persia's religious capital, where their kings were inaugurated; so, a victory full of special significance. Now, to push through his claim to be the King of Kings across all Persia, Alexander needed help from the hand of history. He made many plans, but his biggest obstacle to being enthroned – the elephant in the room, if you will – was that Darius was still alive.

We stayed at Persepolis for more than four months, into April, while Alexander chewed over this monumental problem. He hung on for the New Year festival, hoping that the Persian nobility would come to pay him homage as the king. But, except for the Persians he had already appointed as satraps, only a few visitors came. One of them was Phrasaortes, the newly appointed satrap of Persis, who would have been in trouble if he hadn't put in an appearance.

With minimal support from the Persian aristocrats, it was war once more. We set off to march to Ecbatana, the northern capital, where Darius was. And now, there was a new mood in the army and among the commanders.

Lysander told me that the Macedonian officers saw this pursuit as a huge risk: to search for an enemy who would certainly move to the eastern part of the Persian empire. Unless Darius stood his ground at Ecbatana (and he was not celebrated for standing and fighting on any ground), our army would be forced to follow him to unknown countries, fighting an entirely new kind of war, of which we knew nothing.

Before we left Persepolis, there took place one of the most shameful burnings that I have ever witnessed. There were many different accounts, all with the luxury of hindsight. Some say that Alexander ordered it as retribution for the burning of Athens by the Persians many years ago. Others, that it was the upshot of a drunken party. Still more commentators say that the fire was planned to damage, but not destroy, precisely three buildings: these were the palace of Xerxes, who had razed Athens to the ground, but not the palace of Darius, who hadn't wrecked anything, except his own chances; the throne room (the apadana); and the treasury. I am in favour of this last theory, especially in the light of the restorations that Alexander ordered when he came back to Persepolis. But the fact remained that our leader could not afford to allow the Persians to regroup at Persepolis before he went again in pursuit of Darius.

We marched north-west, crossing Deh Bid pass, and in June we reached Ecbatana, the capital of the satrapy Media. But, only two days before, just as we had feared, Darius had gone to the east. He had stayed at Ecbatana during the winter, hoping to be reinforced, while Alexander lingered in Persepolis. It seems that Darius' soldiers arrived too late. From now on, he was no longer fighting to regain his empire. The King of Kings was fighting for his survival, and hoping to be in Bactria before our Macedonian army could overtake him.

Behind Darius, support was collapsing. A prince named Bisthanes, the son of the former king Artaxerxes the Third, surrendered Ecbatana to our army. This was the last of Persia's royal capitals to be captured. Alexander continued his policy of luring Persian noblemen away from his opponent; a Persian named Atropates was later appointed as satrap of Media, the region of which Ecbatana was capital.

Darius was taking with him the treasure of Ecbatana, so he was travelling slowly. His only hope now was to reach the eastern satrapies and recruit an army. So he continued east, to Parthia, and onwards to Bactria.

The eastern region of Bactria was the ancient Persian heartland; the satrap (ruler) of Bactria, Bessus, was the most important man in the Persian empire, after the king. It was customary for a crown prince to reign in Bactria for a couple of years, as part of his kingly education; and a king without grown-up sons – as was Darius – would appoint his brother or another male relative as ruler in this satrapy. So Bessus was possibly very closely related to Darius; the more reason for the king to think himself safe when he reached Bessus' territory. Still more so, because Bessus had been Darius' chief commander at the battle of Gaugamela.

To Bessus and his allies, however, the situation must have been clear: if they remained loyal to Darius, the Macedonians would invade the eastern satrapies. If they arrested Darius and delivered him to the Macedonians, there would be no war. They felt it was unlikely that the Macedonians were interested in unknown countries, where they would have to fight a war in conditions they had never encountered before.

Alexander pursued Darius with his mounted archers and cavalry at breakneck speed. After twelve days, we were at Rhagae, where he ordered a brief rest while the infantry caught up with us. Two days later, we crossed the pass known as the Caspian Gate and reached Parthia. Here, Alexander was met by two servants of Darius – one of them being the son of the re-appointed satrap of Babylonia, Mazaeus. They told him that Darius had been arrested by Bessus, who was offering to hand over the king to Alexander.

This creates a conundrum of unprecedented proportions for Alexander. As we rest that night by the campfire, Lysander and I discuss the options, and the potential consequences. And, although we are both the offspring of kings, he is far more aware than I am of what those consequences could be. At first, I'm all for what seems the simple solution. 'Why can't he just accept Bessus' offer?'

He takes a stick and stirs the sparks until they fly in the dark. 'If he does that, he will also have to accept the independence of the eastern half of the empire; that runs counter to the aims of his entire crusade. But it's worse than just that…'

'Go on.'

'Alexander will also have to make a decision about what happens to Darius. If he kills him, he will never be accepted by the Persians. And the territories he's conquered will never be secure. If Alexander spares Darius, he would win the loyalty of the Persians, but this loyalty could always revert to the former king.'

'And if he doesn't accept Bessus' offer?'

'Bessus will kill Darius and become king himself.'

'In which case, Alexander could win the loyalty of the Persians by launching a crusade against the regicide?'

'You have it, my lady.'

I gaze at the flames of the fire as they slowly die down. 'So it would seem that Alexander's reassurances to the wife and family of Darius after the battle of Issus – that he sought only dominion, not blood – were in vain. He cannot have dominion without blood, even if he is not the one who spills it.'

'Alexander said it himself, did he not? There can never be two suns.'

In the event, Alexander decided not to negotiate. After the brief rest, we pressed onwards through the night and at noon the following day reached a village where, he was informed, the captors of Darius had stopped the previous day. His informants told him that there was a short-cut through which he could catch up with them, although it was through uninhabited country where water was scarce. Instantly, Alexander signals to me and Lysander to follow with him, doubtless remembering my black Arabian's skill at finding water when we were crossing the Egyptian desert. Then, knowing that the pace will be too much for his infantry, he dismounts around five hundred cavalrymen and mounts in their place the toughest and fittest officers of his infantry, ordering them to keep their own arms and equipment. The rest of the infantry were to follow in their regular formation.

We set off at dusk, creating storm clouds of sand as we gallop across the desert, covering fifty miles during the night. Just as dawn is breaking, we see another cloud of dust on the horizon. Our prey, Bessus with around six hundred horsemen, is straggling along, escorting a wagon which must be carrying Darius. When they see that it is Alexander himself who is upon them, only a few in the contingent make any offer of resistance; after losing a few men, they make off. During the skirmishing, we see Bessus and his allies try at first to get the wagon away, then they give up and make their escape. When Alexander finally catches up with the enemy he has been pursuing for so long, he finds that Darius has eluded him after all. The King of Kings is dead, struck down by the man he went to for help.

*

Alexander gave Darius a state funeral at Persepolis. He gave orders to restore the palace that had been set on fire. And, a few weeks after he had sent part of his army back to Greece, he declared a new war to punish the regicides.

This was received with very mixed feelings by his previously staunchly loyal troops. Many of the Macedonian soldiers had been under arms for twenty years, or even longer. They yearned for their homes, and they disliked the new campaign, which was being conducted, as they saw it, purely for the benefit of the Persians. They had not marched five thousand miles, fought three major battles, four protracted and bloody sieges, and countless skirmishes for this.

Lysander joins me one evening, while the Myrmidons are the supper guests of his cavalry. We walk through the streets of Persepolis, with showers of meteorites sparkling overhead and a dry, hot breeze blowing in from the desert. Seeing no one particularly paying attention to us, I slip my hand into his; it closes warmly around mine. I say quietly to him, 'When do you think we can go home?'

He replies in a low voice, 'This eastern war is necessary if there is to be peace in the west; but whether you and I and our soldiers are under any obligation to be part of it, my lady, is a different question.'

'I know that Alexander needs the support of the Persian aristocrats, and he will only get that if he becomes their king…'

'Which obliges him to avenge the death of Darius. But there is more to it than that. No one could claim to be the successor of the Persian kings if he did not control Bactria and Sogdia; these eastern satrapies are the most ancient and important in the Persian empire.'

'Xanthippe tells me that they also have some of the worst climate extremes – from deathly deserts to freezing, snow-covered mountains.'

'And dangerous warriors. The power of Bessus is based on his mounted archers; they can strike anywhere they want, and are deadly and swift.'

I stop indignantly. 'Excuse me, so are the Myrmidons!'

He laughs quietly, slipping us into the shadows, his

arms round me. 'Then, I think, my lady, that you have just answered both of our questions.'

*

Before we could make a move towards the eastern satrapies, we had to invade Hyrcania, the tropical region south-east of the Caspian sea. If it was taken by Bessus, it would allow him to attack Alexander's lines of communication when we were marching east. Alexander sent two battalion commanders of the phalanx, Craterus and Coenus, who easily defeated the mountain tribes known as the Tapurians and the Mardians. To govern Hyrcania, Alexander chose his new satrap with care; he picked a Parthian, Amminapes, who had lived at the Macedonian court during Alexander's youth. Amminapes had also been responsible for the surrender of Egypt.

This was clever of Alexander, because he had caused some disapproval among his native Macedonians by dressing along Persian lines since entering this country; how desperately he wanted to please everyone – and what an impossibility that was. But now it was clear that Alexander seriously wanted to punish Bessus for murdering King Darius, many previous adherents of Darius came over to him. Some very influential Persians were now at the royal court in Persepolis as firm allies of Alexander; most of them were also bilingual, which helped to smooth over the many mistakes he made. One of the most cringe-making was that Alexander's portraits, on coins and in sculpture, were extremely offensive to his new subjects. They showed the new king as Heracles, wearing a lion's pelt. According to the Zoroastrian religious beliefs of the Persians, this portrayed him as one of the helpers of *Angra Mainyu*, 'the hostile spirit'; *Angra Mainyu* was the personification of evil, and the eternal opponent of *Ahuramazda*, the personification of light and good. This was probably Alexander's worst-ever PR decision.

*

After securing Hyrcania, the next stage in the eastern war was the march along the road through Parthia towards Bactria and then Sogdia, those most ancient and important regions of the Persian empire. And this is where a bold and clever strategy devised by Lysander at last gave us Myrmidons a bit more to do.

The shortest and easiest way to Bactria was the road through the Kara Kum desert to the Oasis Margiana and on to Bactria. The downside was that travellers, including invading armies, were exposed to the attacks of Bessus' mounted archers. The other road was a lengthy and very punishing detour: through the scorching deserts of Aria, Drangiana, Arachosa, and Gandara, and then across the freezing Hindu Kush mountains.

Lysander told me about the meeting with Alexander and his top generals, where the strategy was discussed. 'I thought, when one of the older generals suggested going the long way round, that Alexander would be flatly against it. But he was in favour.'

'Doesn't sound like his usual, headlong self.'

'Not in the least.'

'So, was everyone else in favour, too?'

'I could see that not everyone was. So, with my usual infinite tact and delicacy—'

'And modesty!'

'I reminded him of his secret weapon. How the Myrmidons were perfect for tackling Bessus' mounted archers and their guerrilla-style warfare. And how effectively they had been the cutting edge of our cavalry on countless occasions.'

'What was his reaction?'

'I could see most of the generals nodding in agreement. And, credit to him, Alexander heard me out. Then, he said, "I concede that the Myrmidons have surpassed expectations more than once. They lack nothing in valour. But I would not like to risk these gallant warriors being harmed." Those were his exact words.'

'What did you say in reply?'

'I kept it fact-based. That you were well protected by Spartan armour, as are your horses. That you had the benefit of deadly Spartan arrows. And, to cap it all, a superior power-to-weight ratio – which was what gave you the edge on speed at the Olympics.'

'And?'

'He was fascinated by my last point. Loved "power-to-weight ratio"!'

'That was always my father's favourite argument.'

'It carried the day. The meeting ended with Alexander in very jovial mood, joking that his cavalrymen would all have to lose weight to improve their speed!'

I AM LYDIA

*

I did suggest to Lysander that we train up many more mounted archers before setting out to meet Bessus, and Alexander was in total accord. So by the time that our army trotted out onto the road towards the Kara Kum desert, our Myrmidons were supported by two hundred male mounted archers, all armed with our now-famous arrows. They weren't as fast as the Myrmidons because of the P-to-W ratio, but they were extremely accurate. And behind us were Lysander's cavalry and several more mounted cohorts in a key position to charge down and make the most of the slaughter we would deal. We didn't have the foot soldiers with us – there was no point in the phalanx, when the enemy you're up against is riding horses and firing arrows.

None of the Myrmidons liked the sound of Bessus' mounted archers. So we were in a tough mood when we saw the first signs of dust on the desert plains. They were spread out for maybe a half mile across the horizon. I have a quick word with Lysander: 'If we hit at their flanks and their rear, you can charge and break their line in the centre?'

He nods. 'That'll work.' He passes quick orders to the cavalry, while we divide ourselves into two squadrons and gallop at breakneck speed to take Bessus from his sides and rear. They must have guessed our purpose, but, as my father says, you can't start a rearguard action when you're advancing into battle.

Once we're behind the enemy ranks, we wait until the Bessus mounted archers start to attack our cavalry. Then, we close on their flanks and rear with relentless arrow storms. Their numbers are greater than ours, but our repeated, headlong attacks come as a total surprise. Then our cavalry makes an all-out charge, hurling deadly accurate spears before closing with lethal hand-to-hand combat on horseback. Bessus' men are not used to this cool, planned ferocity. In less than an hour, they've fled, or they're dead. We have six cavalrymen who have sustained thigh wounds from enemy arrows, but they'll live.

When the main army catches up with us, Lysander reports to Alexander. Satisfied that, if Bessus' mounted archers return for another go, we have the means to deal with them, he orders the march through the desert to the Oasis Margiana, and from there, onwards to Bactria. At the oasis, we are joined by reinforcements, making Alexander's army now sixty thousand strong. Marching into the ancient Persian heartlands, to call the regicide Bessus to account, so that Alexander can finally sit on the throne of the King of Kings.

EIGHT

'THE PERSIAN POWER IS IN THE DUST'
Aeschylus, *The Persians*

As Bactria's desert heat slowly gives way to snow-covered mountains, and we climb ever higher, we have to abandon the wagons that the reinforcements have brought and use only pack animals. Even then, the poor beasts frequently slip on the icy paths and sometimes have to be slaughtered. This is hostile territory that we have never encountered before, and I cannot say truthfully that we are well prepared for it. Our army tunics and cloaks are woefully inadequate as protection against the biting wind; at night, the Myrmidons sleep with their horses, which are, at least, kept well fed from Alexander's supply train.

Finally over the mountains, we plunge back into extreme heat again, on the march to the River Oxus, across nearly fifty miles of waterless desert. It is too hot to travel by day, so we walk at night. And this time, it is a death march. Some of the weaker soldiers, who are still recovering from wounds, cannot take the deprivation of water, and they die from dehydration. When Alexander is offered water, from an old man who has brought it for his soldier sons, he staunchly tells him to give it to the sons; he wishes to share the hardships of the rank and file.

But worse is to come, and it shows how inexperience can kill. When our army finally gets to the River Oxus, many men die from uncontrolled drinking. This is pitiful to see, when clear orders from their officers to regulate their intake would have avoided these tragic deaths.

The Oxus is a mighty river, fifteen hundred miles long and several hundred yards wide, drawing its water from the melting ice of the mountains and draining northwards into the inland Aral sea. Most of it is navigable, although Bessus has done his best to try and prevent us from crossing by burning all available boats. Undeterred, the soldiers make rafts by stuffing animal skins and tents with hay. Five days later, we're on the far bank, having crossed from Bactria to Sogdia.

When Bessus' men see that tens of thousands of soldiers are prepared to cross freezing mountains, hellish deserts, and one of the largest rivers in Asia in order to call their leader to account, they are completely demoralised, and his support melts away like ice in the sun. Two of Bessus' courtiers, Spitamenes and Datames, arrest him and deliver him to Alexander. What happens next is too horrible to describe, so I will spare you the detail. Suffice it to say that

Bessus was cruelly mutilated; it was what Alexander had to do as a Persian king punishing a regicide. Bessus was then handed over to Darius' brother, Oxyathres. Alexander ordered Oxyathres to bring Bessus to the desert place where he had killed King Darius, execute him, and deny his corpse the Persian death rites; I won't say what those are, but it is the equivalent of the Greek denial of burial.

This gruesome avenging completed the whole tortuous saga, which began when Bessus decided to bring his king's life to an end. It was a decision made in panic, that finished in blood and gore, and caused the unnecessary deaths of many men. But, nearly five years after the battle of the Granicus, Alexander's triumph seemed complete; there was now no one left to challenge him as the king of Persia.

The evening before we're due to start marching to secure the northern border of Alexander's empire, Lysander and I watch the sparks in our campfire while we discuss regicide. 'My father said that he first heard of the plot to kill the Spartan king Phidias when he was working in the forge.'

He nods. 'That would have been when my father was the leader of the Krypteia.'

'And my father was a spy for the Krypteia.'

Lysander smiles. 'He seems to have been rather a good one!'

'All the same, it was a plot that nearly killed your father, as well as poor old King Phidias.'

The flames illuminate Lysander's pale hair as he shoves a stick into the fire. 'But look at the bloodshed that Bessus has caused! And yet, it had to be this way. It had to be a Persian who killed Darius.'

'So that avenging him would legitimise Alexander's claim to the throne. But it was a horrible punishment, even for a regicide.'

He replies, 'Whereas our ephors got the Persians to do the punishing for them.'

'I can hardly believe that Erastus thought he would get a hero's welcome when he arrived in Babylon. But that's what Erebos said.'

'And my mother told me that the people of Sparta were actually calling for our fathers to become the new kings. The army, too. That's more than they seem to be doing for Alexander!' Lysander gets up. 'That's why we're heading north tomorrow; there are certain to be pockets of resistance. Time to check the horses.'

I stand, with the familiar tug at my insides, as the space between us starts to widen. Then, something snaps. I go to him, hold him as tightly as I can, and whisper, 'When we get back to Sparta, will you marry me? Because I think I might die if you don't!'

His embrace is so strong, it takes my breath away. We do check the horses, eventually.

*

The next day sees us marching across the dusty steppe country of Sogdiana; I'm glad that we have only minor skirmishes on the way, because the phalanx couldn't operate in this hilly terrain.

After nearly two hundred miles, we reach Maracanda, where Alexander establishes a garrison. The people there seem merely curious at this vast army, and I wonder how much they know about the political turmoil that has been gripping neighbouring Bactria. But Alexander is in a hurry to press on to the northernmost river of his new realm, the Jaxartes. Lysander tells me that Alexander's teacher, Aristotle, had told him that the Jaxartes originated in the Hindu Kush mountains, from where it sent off a branch stream that became the River Tanais. This river is generally acknowledged to be the border between Asia and Europe; hence, Alexander could genuinely claim to have reached the 'end of Asia'.

So it is on the southern shoreline of the River Jaxartes that Alexander founds a new city, called Alexandria Eschatê – 'the furthest Alexandria'. Its purpose is to be a garrison against the nomadic tribes that roam north of the river, the Scythians. It replaces an older city called Cyreschata or Cyropolis, which was named after Cyrus the Great, the founder of the first Persian empire, hundreds of years ago.

Exactly five years after the battle of the Granicus, the foundation of Alexandria-the-Furthest near the edge of the known earth appears to be the final flourish to Alexander's Persian crusade. I can hear you saying, 'Bet it isn't,' and you're right. Because some unwelcome news arrives: Spitamenes – who, you remember, handed his leader Bessus over to Alexander – is now himself at the head of a Sogdian revolt. At first, it appears that our army is the cause. Apparently, one of our cavalry commanders, Stasanor, had tried to put an end to the religious custom of exposing the dead to dogs and vultures. Another violation of religious practice is that our army must have appropriated cows. This, apparently, is

'THE PERSIAN POWER IS IN THE DUST'

the only sin that is explicitly condemned in the Zoroastrian creed, which is the prevailing religion in Sogdia.

But the real, bitter reason for the revolt was the founding of Alexandria-the-Furthest; it was one of Alexander's most terrible mistakes. For many years, the native Sogdians south of the River Jaxartes and the nomadic Scythians to the north had lived in harmony. Now, Alexander's creation of the new frontier, with the garrisoned city to watch over it, threatened this historical bond. Turning on Alexander, Sogdians and Scythians joined forces to wage a vicious guerrilla war.

Far from being the end of Alexander's campaign, this uprising marked the beginning of an entirely new kind of warfare. Because the Sogdians and the Scythians are all extremely good mounted archers. Not as fast as the Myrmidons but vastly outnumbering us, even allowing for the two hundred extra mounted archers we trained up to take on Bessus' men.

In lightning-quick time, even for him, Alexander is forced to reorganise his cavalry and recruit Persian horsemen. As he had already appointed Persians as satraps, and had Persian courtiers, the introduction of native soldiers was in fact a logical next step, even though he had no choice in the matter.

This series of uprisings was a far cry from the previous staged battles, where everyone had a chance to prepare for their entrance. This was chaos; so, while Alexander strove to take the initiative by completely overwhelming seven Sogdian forts, Spitamenes' horsemen were besieging the garrison at Maracanda. When our army started to march back to relieve the garrison, the Scythians attacked us in the rear. Then came the worst military disaster of Alexander's career. He decided to return to the offensive in Sogdia, while sending two thousand Greek infantry and three hundred cavalry to Maracanda. They were completely annihilated by Spitamenes' horsemen.

While 2,300 of his men were being wiped out at Maracanda, Alexander crossed the Jaxartes and defeated the Scythians, in what was arguably his most spectacular victory ever. He followed it up by ravaging a part of Sogdia; its peasants would never again support the rebellion, because there were no peasants left. Having obtained the surrender of the northern rebels, he rode south again, covering 180 miles in three days with his cavalry. Maracanda was relieved, but Spitamenes – without doubt, Alexander's most dangerous and intractable enemy – had escaped.

We spent the winter at Balkh, the capital of Bactria, waiting for reinforcements. Our army was never smaller than at this stage. And when the reinforcements did arrive, they were Greek mercenaries, not Macedonians. Alexander had drained the famous Macedonian manpower and made his own country militarily weak.

With his own military strength now reinforced, Alexander divided his army: two thirds were to defend Bactria, and the remainder were to go north and build garrison towns. I was relieved when Lysander and I found that my Myrmidons and his cavalry were to remain in Bactria.

But a decision of Alexander's as to the garrison towns led to one of the greatest mistakes of his life. He had

'THE PERSIAN POWER IS IN THE DUST'

decided to assign control of the troublesome province of Sogdia to Cleitus 'the Black' – a loyal, veteran cavalry commander who had, on one occasion, saved Alexander's life. Understandably, Cleitus was not overjoyed at the prospect of managing a rebellious region on the far edge of the known world.

The night before Cleitus was due to take up his post, Alexander held a banquet in Maracanda, and the wine flowed. Many courtiers were flattering the conquering hero, who had almost won the war in the desert. Some called him the son of Zeus and belittled Alexander's human father, Philip. Others made jokes about the commanders who had been defeated and killed by Spitamenes. This was more than Cleitus could stomach; he had served under Philip, and he had known the dead commanders. He started to praise Philip and criticise Alexander.

The final straw was when Cleitus mocked the young king's adoption of certain Persian practices, such as the wearing of a diadem and Persian clothes. What particularly disgusted Cleitus – and the Macedonians in general – was Alexander's attempts to have his subjects prostrate themselves on greeting him. No Greek bows the knee to anyone who is not a god.

This threw Alexander into a blood-rage. Pushing aside his bodyguards, he hurled a spear at Cleitus, killing him instantly. When Alexander sobered up, he knew that he had made a terrible and irreversible mistake. Lysander, who has read Aristotle, Alexander's tutor and mentor, quoted to me from his work: '*One who sins when drunk, must be punished twice: once for sinning, and once for being drunk.*'

For three days, Alexander refused to drink a single drop of water, which brought him close enough to death. What brought him round were the slithery sayings of a philosopher (so called) named Anaxarchus of Abdera; this Anaxarchus told Alexander that the king is (like Zeus) justice personified, and can therefore not act badly. This set a new standard of flattery at Alexander's court. From now on, hardly anyone dared to correct him.

*

When the northern garrisons had been established, the two armies were re-united in Balkh, and Alexander made some major changes. Firstly, he recruited thirty thousand young Persians to form a phalanx. He also added local cavalry units to the Macedonian army; Persian mounted archers were to play an important role in the coming years. This caused great tensions among the Macedonian troops, who had followed and fought for him for so long. Although they were longing for their homeland, they felt rejected and humiliated; was this to be their reward for putting their lives on the line, battle after battle, year after year, for their young king?

With his general Coenus in hot pursuit of the endlessly troublesome rebel Spitamenes, Alexander turned his attention to the last outpost of rebellion in the eastern state of Sogdia. A powerful Sogdian chief, named Oxyartes, refused to submit to Alexander and had taken refuge in a mountain fort, the Sogdian Rock. He had provisioned it well, was supported by a large number of natives, and had chosen this refuge for his wife and family, in the belief that the Rock was impregnable. This was the last stronghold of Sogdia; should it fall, there would be nowhere to go for those who still offered resistance.

When we reached the Rock, it looked like an impossibility, rising sheer on every side. Deep snow on the summit made the ascent even more difficult and guaranteed the defenders a supply of water. But Alexander's determination had been hardened to steel by an insult from the defenders. He had called on them to discuss terms, offering to allow them to return unharmed to their homes if they surrendered the stronghold. Their answer was a shout of laughter. They told Alexander to find soldiers with wings to capture the Rock for him, as no other mortal caused them any concern.

Seething with anger, Alexander turned the assault into a competition; he proclaimed that he would give a prize of twelve talents to the first man up, eleven to the second, and ten to the third; and so on to the twelfth, who would receive three hundred gold darics. Now, when you consider that just one talent was the amount of silver needed to pay the entire crew of a trireme (around 180 marines) for a month, we are talking shiploads of money. To their credit, the men were already very keen, but these rewards were an added spur.

Our army had around three hundred men who had experience in rock-climbing from previous sieges. They had provided themselves with small iron tent pegs to drive into the snow where it was frozen hard, or into any bare earth they might encounter, and they had attached strong, flaxen lines to the pegs. These intrepid climbers set off under cover of darkness to the steepest part of the rock face, as this was the least likely to be guarded. Then began the daunting ascent, up sheer rock, in the dark, with nothing to save them if they fell.

Thirty men fell to their death during the ascent, and their bodies were never recovered from the snow. The remaining ninety per cent of these heroes reached the top of the Rock, as dawn was breaking. Following Alexander's orders, they signalled their success to the troops below by waving linen flags. Alexander sent a crier to shout the news to the enemy's advanced posts, that they could now surrender without further delay, as the men with wings had been found and were already in possession of the summit.

This was the last news the defenders were expecting. Shocked to the core, they were so alarmed by the 270 Macedonian troops they could see that they imagined that a large, fully armed force must be in possession. Their surrender was immediate. Many women and children were among the prisoners, including the wife and daughters of the rebel leader, Oxyartes.

One of his daughters was called Roxane, and I had to agree with Lysander that, apart from the wife of Darius, she was the most beautiful woman we had seen in Asia. Alexander was totally smitten from first sight. So it was a love-match, as well as a politically good move to restore some stability to the region, when he married her.

Political necessity or not, it was also cruel. Alexander already had a Persian mistress, Barsine, and she had recently borne him a son, Heracles. The marriage to Roxane was also an insult to Barsine's father, Artabazus, who had played a very important role during the past three years in attracting the Persian elite to Alexander's side, and in the various revolts and the war against Spitamenes. Barsine was sent away; both she and her father deserved better.

The end of Spitamenes himself was precipitated by the taking of the Oasis Margiana by Alexander's General Craterus, which cut off the rebel from an essential water supply. Then, General Coenus caught up with him and defeated him. On seeing this, Spitamenes' own people killed him and sued for peace. I will spare you the detail of how they killed him.

But large pockets of resistance still remained in these eastern regions. So, when our army finally departed Bactria and Sogdia, an enormous garrison of at least eleven thousand men was left to keep the fragile peace. Meanwhile, we continued east, over the Hindu Kush mountains, into an entirely unknown world. And I began to ask myself seriously why we were still following Alexander, when Persia had been won.

NINE

'THE SOULS OF MIGHTY CHIEFS UNTIMELY SLAIN'
The *Iliad*, Book 1

After the dreary steppe country of Bactria and Sogdia, the long trek through the Hindu Kush mountains is a journey of wonders. We're travelling in summer, so avoiding the heavy snowfall and freezing temperatures of winter. And after our experiences searching for water in the burning heat of the desert, the frequent rainfall is like a gift from the gods. On the higher peaks that tower above us, we can see heavy cloaks of snow that must last all year round. Once, Lysander points upwards at a strange phenomenon on the snowy heights. I shade my eyes from the sun to try and make out the shapes. 'It looks like kneeling human figures – but it can't be, can it?'

He smiles. 'Snow men? I don't think so. Could be an effect of the wind, perhaps.'

There is abundant wildlife in the mountains; mountain goats do breathtaking dances across the crags, and sometimes we spot wild sheep. Vultures and majestic eagles soar overhead. And when we cross streams, we can see that they're bubbling with brown trout. Lysander says that black and brown bears live in caves and hunt here but are too shy to come near our vast army columns.

As we start to descend, the lower slopes are undulating grassland, which our horses make a good meal of when we make camp. Lysander tells me over our campfire that tomorrow we enter the western valley of the mighty River Indus, where the Persians still rule. This comes as a surprise to me. 'So… that's why we're here, is it? To kick the Persians out?'

He hesitates. 'I had reports from Erebos that there were Indians from the Gandara region – that's the area west of the Indus – who were fighting under Darius at Gaugamela.'

'I wonder if any of the poor devils lived to go home!'

He pauses, staring into the flames. Then he turns to me. 'If you're asking me whether I think we should be here, my lady, the answer is no, I don't.'

'But right now, we have no choice, do we?'

'We can't do anything that could affect the morale of troops who could well be thinking the same thoughts as we are.'

'Especially now that Alexander has recruited so many Persians into the ranks!'

'He has run out of Macedonians and has dwindling supplies of Greek mercenaries.'

'All the more reason to head home.'

Lysander says softly, 'But you and I know, my lady, that reason is not what drives Alexander.'

*

As we descended into the Indus valley, we saw that this beautiful goddess of a river fed the crops and cattle of many people. The people themselves looked poor but happy, and there was no sign of Persian oppression. They were welcoming to Alexander; once, when he had been bitten by a snake, and his own physicians were powerless to help, some Indian healers came forward. Not only could they fix the snake bite: they were also able to cure other diseases and painful conditions. In fact, they were such good physicians that he took some of them with him on his Indian campaign.

You'd think that this kindness might engender feelings of gratitude in whatever Alexander had inside his chest that passed for a heart. But as far as he was concerned, he was simply taking possession of territories which he had wrested from the Persians and now considered rightfully his own. So his next step was to invite all the chieftains of the former Persian satrapy of Gandara to come to him and submit to his authority. First came a chief, Omphis, ruler of a kingdom called Taxila, which extended eastwards from the Indus to the Hydaspes river. Omphis was also last because no one followed him. And so began Alexander's Indian campaign.

*

'THE SOULS OF MIGHTY CHIEFS UNTIMELY SLAIN'

There were many chieftains who put up a fierce resistance to Alexander's army. Can you blame them? In their eyes, he was no better than the Persians, who had tried – and miserably failed – to take the whole of India. Now here was another King of Kings, who was following in the same footsteps.

What made it worse was Alexander's criminal lack of scruples or honour. When he was lightly wounded during the siege of a hill fortress, which we took, all the defenders were massacred. In another valley, the terrorised population fled, after setting fire to their own villages. A truly shocking event was when, during a cold night, our troops burned the small wooden boxes they found in a town they were besieging. The boxes turned out to be coffins: a sacrilege considerably more awful than when the Persians slaughtered the Apis bull during their invasions of Egypt.

A betrayal, that will sicken you as much as it does me, took place when the capital of the Assacenes tribe, a town called Massaga, surrendered. This was only after Cleophis, the old mother of the fallen chieftain of Massaga, had assumed supreme command of their army, and the entire population of local women joined in the fighting. Alexander demanded that the mercenaries who had defended the town join his own army. So they placed themselves at his mercy, and were exterminated. He went on to slaughter the entire population of Massaga and reduced its buildings to rubble. A similar slaughter followed at Ora, another stronghold of the Assacenes.

Lysander considered that Alexander's campaign through this area was, in fact, genocide; I don't think that's too strong a word. Alexander wasn't waging a war; he was committing war crimes. It was shocking and shameful to be part of this butchery.

*

It's a now-familiar theme of each campaign, whether in Persia, Egypt, or India, that Alexander does something that – to him – has religious significance, connected with his ancestry. And quite often, too, reveals his lack of understanding of the local gods, which would be comical if it wasn't pitiful, and insulting to the indigenous people. In the Indian campaign, this involved Alexander taking Hephaestion, me, Lysander, and our cohorts to visit a place called Nysa. It's a humble collection of huts, with the backdrop of a magnificent mountain, its crest wreathed in wispy clouds.

As we look on, saluting at appropriate times, I whisper to Lysander, 'Who is he pouring libations to?'

He whispers back, 'Dionysus, god of ecstasy, one of his mythological ancestors.'

'So, is Dionysus identified with some Indian god, like Zeus was with Ammon in Egypt?'

'He thinks the mountain is called *Meros*, which in Greek means *thigh*. He likes this, because of the story that Dionysus was born from Zeus' thigh, biologically strange though that may be.'

'He *thinks*.'

'He thinks wrong. The Indian name is *Meru*, meaning the holy mountain, or "axis" of the world.'

'THE SOULS OF MIGHTY CHIEFS UNTIMELY SLAIN'

At this point, I'm taken with such a fit of laughter at the idea of Zeus giving birth via his thigh that I'm in danger of breaking a rib trying to contain it. Lysander sees me shaking and has to look away, suppressing a smile. Even on the way back, I keep murmuring to myself, 'Biologically strange though that may be,' and it sets me off again.

*

After the carnage and arson in Massaga and Ora, we march across the Shang-La pass and approach the mighty Indus. The many people who Alexander had terrorised had fled to a high mountain fortress called Aornus, meaning 'hiding place' in Indian. According to local legend, not even the god Krishna – who was identified by the Macedonians with Heracles, another of Alexander's many mythical ancestors – had been able to take this rock. Rising 5,600 feet above the river, and with a deep ravine on its more vulnerable north side, it was to be Alexander's final really big siege. Lysander told me that the military thinking was that Aornus presented a threat to Alexander's supply line, which stretched over the Hindu Kush back to Balkh in Bactria. Although privately, he and I agreed that a hiding place full of terrified villagers hardly presented a military menace; we think Alexander was just missing the good old days of pummelling walls and humans to pieces.

Neighbouring tribesmen, who had surrendered, showed him the best point of access; then began the task of building an earthwork that would bridge the ravine in order to bring the siege engines within reach. At first, the siege engineers were attacked by boulders rolled down from on high. This initial repulse was celebrated by the defenders with three days of drumbeats. Having given everyone a headache, they then, surprisingly, retreated. Alexander, in his usual flamboyant style, hauled himself up the last rock face on a rope, slaughtered any fugitives he could, and proceeded to erect altars to Athena Nike (Athena of Victory). A local chieftain, Sisikottos, who had helped Alexander in this campaign, was made the governor of Aornus.

*

Having secured his back, Alexander now turned to the friendly governor of Taxila, Omphis, who was looking for support against his neighbour, Porus. And now approached a battle which was to be a game-changer for Alexander. First, some backstory on Porus, because he deserves our respect. This man is a regional king in India, famed for his personal strength and noble courage. At six foot seven inches tall, he is a considerably mightier warrior than Alexander. And his army is formidable.

To begin with, you have his archers; carrying a bow as tall as themselves, they rest the base on the ground, and their left foot fires arrows that are not far short of ten feet long. Nothing can resist an Indian archer's shot, neither shield nor breastplate. So don't get in the way of one.

Then, there are the war elephants. They are huge and powerful, and trained to kill. Whether it's by simply trampling people beneath their feet, crushing their armour and their bones. Or by lifting the victim high in the air with their trunks and dashing them violently to the ground. Or, they gore them with their tusks. Now, I mentioned before that elephants are, unsurprisingly, dreaded by horses, which have to be specially trained to face them. We've had war elephants looming for a while in this story; it's time to bring them on.

The Jhelum river is another key player in this battle because it is the border between the countries of Porus and Omphis, the two warring neighbours. The weather is also a major factor: in June, the Jhelum river will swell with the melting of the mountain snows, and the advent of the monsoon season. Porus is likely hoping that this is a battle that will never take place if Alexander and his army can't get across the river.

Alexander and his generals knew that they had to act quickly. There was only time to mobilise around half the army for the march to the east. The ships that Alexander had used to cross the Indus had to be carried along the main road to the Jhelum river. The torrent was already flowing deep and fast, and Porus was waiting on the other side. Any opposed crossing would probably doom all of us. So we find another crossing, seventeen miles upstream of our camp; Alexander leaves General Craterus behind with most of the army while he crosses with a strong contingent, including the Myrmidons and his Companion Cavalry, with Lysander and his horsemen.

Seeing the plan, Porus sends a small cavalry and chariot force under his son to where we are crossing. The Myrmidons fire storms of arrows all the way across, to try and protect our men. And from the start of the onslaught, the son of Porus is in trouble, because his chariots are getting bogged down in the rain-soaked mud. But Porus' son must have something deeply personal with Alexander. Because nothing can stop him surging forward to kill Alexander's beloved horse Bucephalus with one blow and then wound our fallen leader.

That's as far as the son of Porus gets before Lysander cuts him down, and Alexander's bodyguards rush him to safety. He's had horses killed under him before, but not the horse he so dearly loves. Bucephalus has been with him for his entire military life, ever since he tamed the big black stallion as a teenager by turning him into the sun, having realised that the animal was afraid of its own shadow. We've never seen him shaken before. But not for long: he hasn't time, because Porus the elder is re-thinking, and launching his entire army at us. They have cavalry on both flanks, the war elephants in front and infantry behind the elephants.

Alexander must have been incandescent with fury by now. He starts the battle by sending his mounted archers, female and male, to shower Porus' left cavalry wing. I can feel the anger of my Myrmidons at the slaughter of Bucephalus, as we launch a deathly hail, our triple-barbed arrows felling the enemy like a forest being blown over in a raging storm. Our cavalry follows up by destroying theirs, hurling their javelins and then dispatching the survivors with one well-placed stab of their swords.

At one point, the Myrmidons draw their swords and go in to help. It's not the first time we've done this, but I have never been so hell-bent on destruction, as I grip the wolf-emblazoned hilt of my father's sword. In Spartan style, it's shorter than the swords used by other Greeks, and it's deadly: capable of being thrust through gaps in armour, with the groin and throat the easiest targets. Now I can hear you saying, 'I thought that rage was forbidden in the Spartan army'; you're right. But it's infinitely worse seeing a noble animal slaughtered than a noble human, because the horse is not there by choice. I'm not trying to excuse our rage, because it's not excusable; anger is a kind of insanity that is best avoided.

While the Myrmidons join in the swordplay, our phalanxes have crossed the river to engage the charge of the war elephants. They don't take on the elephants; they slay the mahouts who are riding them, hurling their eighteen-foot sarissas with a deadly accuracy, while a platoon of foot archers supports them with showers of arrows. As soon as their riders fall, the elephants are in disarray; some slip and crash down into the mud, while others panic and stampede back onto the infantry behind them.

The battle raged on for hours, despite our army vastly outnumbering that of Porus. The enemy must have had abundant reason to be determined, having witnessed the death of their leader's son. But Alexander was impressed by Porus, and did not wish this great and valiant soldier to be killed. So he sent a number of ambassadors to him to try and negotiate terms, finally succeeding with a man named Meroes, who – Alexander was informed – had long been a friend of Porus. In the end, wounded in the shoulder, and with almost his entire army massacred, Porus surrendered and was treated with great dignity (can I hear you saying, 'For once a prisoner is being treated well!'?).

Alexander forced the two warring neighbours, Omphis and Porus, to be reconciled, and appointed Porus as satrap of his own kingdom, which – as in similar past appointments – guaranteed the loyalty of his former aggressor. He founded two cities on opposite sides of the Jhelum river where the battle had raged: Nike, meaning 'victory town', and Bucephala, in honour of his cherished warhorse.

But, as Lysander and I take a rest at our camp by the river, the mud washed off in a quick, cold dip, we're both thinking the same thing: 'Victory or not, this battle has been the hardest we've ever fought!'

He looks up at the monsoon clouds ballooning across the evening sky. 'At least none of our soldiers was felled by archer fire. The mud must have made it impossible for the Indian archers to rest the base of their bow steadily on the ground.'

'But if there's a next time, it could be a very different story!'

He nods. 'That's what the generals are saying, but, not, of course, to Alexander's face. Porus is a minor king compared with the powers further east.'

'I've heard that the warriors they can call upon are in their hundreds of thousands. And our army outnumbered that of Porus, yet we still had to work desperately hard to beat them!'

His face is grave as he looks at me in the dimming light. 'But there's more to it than that, isn't there?'

'Yes. We shouldn't be here. These people weren't oppressed by the Persians. And now – they're being oppressed by Alexander of Macedon!'

'THE SOULS OF MIGHTY CHIEFS UNTIMELY SLAIN'

He reaches across and gently takes my hand, hardly a delicate one, with its fingertips hardened by hundreds of thousands of arrow shots. 'There's yet more to it than that. I want to take you home and marry you, my lady.' He raises my hand to his lips.

*

That night, I begin to wonder if I should have taken that chilly dip in the river, because I wake up aching all over and freezing cold. The rest of the night, I shiver and shake and ache, and can't get back to sleep. Things are no better the next morning. Staggering over to Xanthippe, I say, 'You're in charge today. And don't come near me, in case what I have is catching!'

She takes one look at me and says, 'I'm ordering you back to bed, boss.' Putting a firm arm round me, she almost carries me back. I don't remember lying down; I think I must have passed out. Hallucinatory dreams drag me into a nether-world, populated with monstrous, fire-breathing elephants that tread me into the ground, making me feel like all my bones are breaking. Thirty-foot-long arrows fly straight at me, piercing my limbs and making me writhe in pain. Huge black vultures circle overhead, with harsh cries that seem to split my head open; I stare up at them, wondering if I'm dead and they're coming for my remains. It seems they are, because one of them suddenly drops from the sky, dragon-like claws heading for my face. I put an arm over my head to try and fend it off, and roll to one side. I'm so cold, it's like I'm lying in a snow drift.

Then I have the sensation of being lifted; the vultures must be carrying me off, to tear me to pieces in their cliff-top nest. I'm moving through the air. If only I could wake and escape this dream, I'd find out if I am alive or dead.

But I don't wake up, and the dream turns darker. I'm underground, in some kind of cavern, lying on the banks of a black, turbulent river that's flowing past me. I'm feeling colder than ever. I can't hear the river. Everything is very quiet. I think, if I can just sleep for a while, maybe I'll wake up and I'll be back in the real world again, back to normal. But it's as though I can't move anything, not even my eyelids. I have to keep staring at the river.

Then, with that dark, swirling river in front of my eyes, my ears hear a voice that I know, reading aloud a story that I have treasured ever since I was a little girl. And I know that I am no longer alone; he is with me, and I am going to live:

Thick as the chill snowflakes shed from the hand of Zeus and borne on the keen blasts of the north wind, even so thick did the gleaming helmets, the bossed shields, the strongly plated breastplates, and the ashen spears stream from the ships. The sheen pierced the sky, the whole land was radiant with their flashing armour, and the sound of the tramp of their treading rose from under their feet. In the midst of them all Achilles put on his armour; he gnashed his teeth, his eyes gleamed like fire, for his grief was greater than he could bear. Thus, then, full of fury against the Trojans, did he don the gift of the god, the armour that Hephaestos had made him.

'THE SOULS OF MIGHTY CHIEFS UNTIMELY SLAIN'

> *First he put on the goodly greaves fitted with ancle clasps, and next he put on the breastplate about his chest. He slung the silver-studded sword of bronze about his shoulders, and then took up the shield so great and strong that shone afar with a splendour as of the moon. As the light seen by sailors from out at sea, when men have lit a fire in their homestead high up among the mountains, but the sailors are carried out to sea by wind and storm far from the haven where they would be – even so did the gleam of Achilles' wondrous shield strike up into the heavens. He lifted the redoubtable helmet and set it upon his head, from whence it shone like a star, and the golden plumes which Hephaestos had set thick about the ridge of the helmet waved all around it. Then Achilles made trial of himself in his armour to see whether it fitted him, so that his limbs could play freely under it, and it seemed to buoy him up as though it had been wings.*

Lysander's voice ceases in a whisper. Slowly, I can at last open my eyes, to look at the only face I want to see in this world. My vision is blurred at first, the blue of his eyes intense as I blink in the light. He reaches towards me and lays a gentle hand on my forehead. 'Can you hear me, my lady?'

I nod and manage a smile. He lifts my head and holds a flask of water to my lips. I realise that I have a raging thirst. He warns, 'Not too much! Just small sips.' With difficulty, I pause my drinking, and he lowers my head back to the pillow. Trying to focus my eyes, I gaze at the riot of colour around me; it sharpens into luxurious fabrics draped over rich, gold-adorned furniture. 'You are in Alexander's tent. When he heard how ill you were, he insisted that I bring you here to care for you. He is sharing with Hephaestion.'

My eyes move to the copy of the *Iliad* that he has laid to one side. He says quietly, 'I can't sing like your father. But I wondered if Homer might be able to bring you back. I'm going to give you some more water now. Don't try to talk, you are exhausted.' He lifts my head, and gratefully I drink again.

Suddenly, sunlight blazes into the tent as the door is pulled back, and Alexander's powerful form comes in, almost silently. He moves to the other side of the couch where I am lying and seats himself. Lysander stands, out of respect for his leader, and instinctively I struggle to sit up, but I can't lift even a finger. Alexander shakes his head. 'You must not try to move, Commander. You have been far too close to Hades.' He looks at Lysander. 'She is drinking, as well as awake?'

'Yes, sir. I think your *Iliad* helped to bring her back.'

Alexander nods, with a pleased expression. 'All the same, I will send my best doctor to her, to see if anything else can be done.'

At last, I find my voice, a whisper, 'He is here with me, sir.'

To my relief, after fearing that he could take offence at my words, I realise from Alexander's smile that he thinks I am referring to him, and his medicinal *Iliad*. He stands. 'It is good to have you back in the land of the living, Commander.' Then, again with hardly a sound, he is swiftly gone.

Lysander lifts my head for me to drink again. 'Small sips, remember.' I cannot remember when water tasted so good. Gently, he lowers my head. 'You have been very ill. We feared you were leaving us.'

'I will never leave you.'

He picks up the *Iliad*. 'Soon, I will bring you some food. But first, you need to sleep. Shall I read to you again?'

'Can it be what my father read to his little pupil… when Patroclus is putting on his armour?'

'It certainly can.' He finds the extract that my father told me he read to the little Athenian Lydia, when he was her tutor:

> *As he spoke, Patroclus put on his armour. First he greaved his legs with greaves of good make and fitted with ancle-clasps of silver; after this he donned the cuirass of the son of Aeacus, richly inlaid and studded. He hung his silver-studded sword of bronze about his shoulders, and then his mighty shield. On his comely head he set his helmet, well-wrought, with a crest of horse-hair that nodded menacingly above it. He grasped two redoubtable spears that suited his hands, but he did not take the spear of noble Achilles, so stout and strong, for none other of the Achaeans could wield it, though Achilles could do so easily. This was the ashen spear from Mount Pelion, which Chiron had cut upon a mountain top and had given to Peleus, wherewith to deal out death among heroes. He bade Automedon yoke his horses with all speed, for he was the man whom he held in honour next after Achilles, and on whose support in battle he could rely most firmly. Automedon therefore yoked the fleet horses Xanthos and Balios, steeds that could fly like the wind.*

In a half-doze, I listen to the voice I love most in the world, until the doze becomes a sleep that is mercifully free of dreams. When I wake, the sun has set, and a candle is burning in the tent. Lysander is still at my side, gazing at me, the flame making his pale hair glow.

*

It was weeks before I got most of my strength back. Even then, my energy levels never quite returned to what they had been. And coming so close to death, from a cause other than battle, made me realise that there are some threats that cannot be tackled with a bow and arrows, or the deadliest sword.

We all had a similar realisation with the battle of the River Jhelum: a game-changer, in more ways than one. It showed the army that one day, if we carried on campaigning in India, we would lose, perhaps catastrophically. And I think that the death of his precious warhorse blew the cold winds of mortality into Alexander's face. He himself would have been killed were it not for Lysander's quick action in cutting down the son of Porus. During the course of his 'crusade', he had received countless wounds; his whole body must have been scarred with them. But, as time went on, he seemed to expose himself more and more to danger in his impassioned determination to win. And there would shortly come a time when we all thought he had gone too far towards Hades ever to return.

Things started to come to a head when Alexander wanted to drive further east and cross the Ganges. Then, he learned that the river was over one thousand feet wide and up to one hundred feet deep. Furthermore, that waiting for him on the opposite shore were the kings of the Ganderites and the Praesii, with eighty thousand horsemen, two hundred thousand infantry, eight thousand chariots, and six thousand war elephants. The country they were defending had never been conquered by any foreign king, because they possessed a vast force of the largest-sized elephants, which are dreaded by all other nations because of their overwhelming numbers and strength. This time, Alexander had to concede that he could not win against these numbers. But he still had his eye on the powerful kingdom of Magadha, which lay to the east of Porus' domain. Alexander gave no reason for wishing to add Magadha to his possessions; it had never been occupied by the Persians and had offered him no aggression. But our leader no longer explained why he went to war.

With the Himalayan snows now melted, the monsoon season in full flow, and the rivers swollen, the army was nonetheless ferried across the rivers Acesines and the Hydraotis. We besieged, and took, a town called Sangala. But then, shortly after the summer solstice, there was an eclipse of the moon, an evil omen. When Alexander ordered his army to cross a third river, the Hyphasis, they refused.

They had left Macedonia to punish Persia and, instead, they had conquered it. The Macedonians had seen their king start to behave like a Persian; they had grumbled but tolerated it. They had won significant victories in India, at increasingly great cost to life and limb. They had marched for seventy days, through continuous rain in the full heat of summer, in a campaign that had gone relentlessly on for thousands of days. Now, they were being ordered to fight in faraway Magadha, which had never belonged to the Persian empire and was thought to be situated at the edge of the earth. Lysander and I were staggered at their loyalty, which was only just now wearing thin.

Alexander was furious. He presumably had different ideas as to how he was going to celebrate his thirtieth birthday. But it was General Coenus, who had played a major role in the victory over Porus, who spoke to Alexander on behalf of the warriors, in an address remarkable for its candour and its courage: '*It is time to return to your own country, see your mother, regulate the affairs of the Greeks, and carry to your fatherland these many great victories. Then, if you wish, start afresh on another expedition against these tribes of Indians in the east, or go even further afield. And new Macedonians and Greeks will follow you, young men in place of old, fresh men in place of exhausted ones, and men for whom warfare has no terrors, because up till now, they have had no experience of it, and they will be eager to set out, in hope of future reward.*'

Sensible, gentle, and logical though this reasoning was, it annoyed Alexander, probably because there wasn't an iota of flattery in it. Lysander told me that Alexander broke up the conference. Next day, now in a towering rage, he called the generals together again, saying, '*I intend to advance further, but I will force no Macedonian to accompany me against his will. I only want those who will follow their king of their own accord. Those who wish to return home may do so; they are at liberty to return and carry back word to their*

'THE SOULS OF MIGHTY CHIEFS UNTIMELY SLAIN'

relations that they have returned, having deserted their king in the midst of his enemies.'

This was well below the belt. And while such shameful tactics might have worked before, this time they fell flat. There was a profound silence throughout the camp; the Macedonians were all incensed at his wrath, without being in the least bit changed by it.

So Alexander fell back on his augurs and sacrificed to his gods (I'm not sure which ones) to ask if his further advance eastwards into India was a good idea. This time, the augurs let him down big time: the omens clearly declared it unfavourable to march further east.

As a last resort, he got his oldest and most faithful friends from the Companion Cavalry together. Lysander said Alexander was hoping they would support him simply for old times' sake. Instead, they urged him to return. And, at last, he listened. The good thing was that his PR machine was backing the decision: the gods, not his men, had ordered him to return. The news went round the camp that we were going home.

TEN

THE RETURN

Many veterans were left behind in yet another newly founded Alexandria, on the east bank of that river-too-far, the Hyphasis. They had little hope of ever returning to Macedonia or Greece. Lysander and I felt that this was one of Alexander's cruellest blows to men who had served him so long and so loyally.

Ironically, no sooner had the decision to return been taken than reinforcements arrived, consisting of six thousand cavalry from Thrace and seven thousand infantry. They brought with them twenty-five thousand suits of armour. The arrival of the reinforcements swelled the size of Alexander's army and its train to around one hundred thousand.

Over a late-night supper, Lysander told me that the next question that was hotly debated among the Macedonian high command was which route to take. 'The easiest route, of course, is simply to retrace our steps through the countries of the now-reconciled neighbours, Porus and Omphis.'

'I can guess what you're going to say – Alexander never goes for the easy option!'

'Especially not when it could look like we're returning after a defeat. So we're going by ship.'

'That certainly doesn't sound easy.'

'We have to get to the ships first. That means marching westwards, back to the Hydaspes river; apparently there's a big ship-building operation underway in Nike and Bucephala.'

'I bet he wasn't building ships in his new cities to take his troops home!'

Lysander gives me one of his sunniest smiles. 'You're ahead of me, as usual, my lady. No, it's likely that the ships were originally part of his invasion plans.'

The monsoon season is mercifully over by the time we reach the River Hydaspes in November. Around eight hundred ships are being built, consisting of warships and transport ships. The clever bit is that these ships are being built to be taken apart and put back together again, so that they can be conveyed across the Punjab, which we are aiming to traverse on our way out of India. The word Punjab means 'The Land of Five Waters', because it is crossed by five rivers, all of which are tributaries of the Indus; so if we're going to hop from one watery highway to the next, we need to be able to drag the boats on land.

The rowers are a mixed bunch of Phoenicians, Carians, Cypriots, and Egyptians, and they're very helpful in getting our horses, fodder, and chariots on board. Then Alexander sacrifices to the river gods, to his legendary ancestor, Heracles, and to the Egyptian god, Ammon, and we're finally underway. The fleet is escorted by two armies, commanded by two of the big chiefs of the Macedonian high command, Craterus, and Alexander's faithful friend, Hephaestion, marching along the banks on either side of the River Hydaspes.

The river gods can't have been very happy with Alexander's sacrifice, because ten days into the voyage, disaster strikes. As you probably noticed from my description of the River Ganges, rivers in India are vast waterways – deep, wide, and frequently fast-flowing. And river travel gets particularly interesting where two of these giants meet, especially after months of monsoon rain. At the confluence of the mighty rivers Hydaspes and Acesines, we see waves tossing spray into the air; ahead of us is a roaring maelstrom, which is going to try and suck us into its maw.

We are among the lucky ones who are aboard a transport ship, where the rounded hull allows us to slip without too much trouble through the turbulence. Those in the warships are less fortunate; the double rows of oars cause the lower row to get caught on the riverbank, sending the ships completely out of control. Lysander told me that at one point, Alexander took off his armour, preparing to jump in the water, he was so convinced the ship was going to sink. Many warships were destroyed in that whirlpool, with great loss of life for humans and animals.

It's when our feet are finally back on land, and repairs to the damaged warships are underway, that Lysander is able to enlighten me about the hidden agenda of where we are actually going. The Myrmidons are entertaining his troops at supper when we go for a quiet walk to check on the horses. Pegasus has survived the chaos of the river confluence in very good order and is tucking happily into his fodder. Lysander runs a hand down the foreleg of his handsome bay, Hector, and lifts the hoof. He touches the inside pad of the hoof gently. 'There's some inflammation here. He was limping slightly as I led him off the ship.'

'You know what could help?'

He smiles, a touch of the mischief in his blue eyes. 'Let's look for some, shall we?'

As we search, he tells me what is being planned by the Macedonian high command. 'Alexander has received news that two tribes, previously enemies, are joining forces to prevent us from marching through their territory. The Mallians and the Oxydracians have been trading hostages with each other and moving all their valuables into their fortified cities.'

'How many will they be if they combine their forces?'

'Some ninety thousand infantry, ten thousand cavalry, and nine hundred chariots.'

'So this alliance is the last thing that Alexander wants.'

'He sees it as threatening our line of communications, which is already over-extended, running as it does from Babylon all the way to the Punjab.'

I see the little herb that I'm looking for, growing at the base of a tree, and pounce. 'There's lots here! Let's get a really good supply.'

'Enough for poor old Hector, I hope?'

'If you ask nicely.'

His arms go round me and draw me gently to him as he whispers, 'I was brought up always to ask nicely, my lady.'

*

I might have known that we would have to fight our way out of India. Even if there had not been the Mallians ganging up with the Oxydracians, Alexander would have found someone else to pick a scrap with. And this time, the orders were to take no prisoners. Alarmed at the threat of compromise to our supply lines, he wanted no quarter offered. Mercy wasn't a habit of his anyway; since the start of his Indian campaign, his army had slaughtered many thousands of men, women, and children.

He divided the army into three parts, with Craterus and Hephaestion commanding the two thirds, and himself at the head of the horse archers (Myrmidons and the two hundred males we had trained up), foot archers, half the elite Companion Cavalry, including Lysander's cohort, and a brigade of the phalanx. While the two thirds would proceed down the river, by ship, and on land, Alexander's force would (no prizes for guessing) take the difficult part, which was a forced march directly across the desert, to surprise the Mallians.

Once we had set out, we marched continuously, with only a single half-day halt at an oasis. Our detachment of the army marched forty-five miles in just twenty-four hours, arriving near the city of Kot Kamala at daybreak. Then, Alexander rode ahead with his mounted forces and totally surprised the Mallians, who never dreamed that he would cross the desert. Those who were not massacred retreated into the city. So Alexander created a cordon of cavalry and mounted archers around the town, and waited for his infantry to arrive, with the siege engines. The ferocious slinging power of the torsion catapults did the job once again, and the garrison of two thousand was slaughtered. The two other parts of the army carried out a pincer action to execute any fleeing survivors.

This merciless pattern continued from one Mallian town to the next; at Atari, the citadel was burned, and five thousand Mallians died within its walls. After giving us a single day's rest, Alexander continued to the chief city of the Mallians. Before we got there, we found them, ready to give battle, on the high ground of the western bank of the River Hydraotis. As at the Granicus and Issus, Alexander made his customary charge across the river, Myrmidons firing from his right flank and cavalry hot on our heels behind, infantry waiting to advance, if necessary. It wasn't: the Mallians fled without our infantry joining battle. We pursued them for five miles, and then they must have realised what a small force we were, compared with what a large one – at fifty thousand strong – they were. So they decided to stop and fight. And we realised how vulnerable we were, with our light infantry nowhere near.

This was the first dangerous mistake. It was a sign of Alexander's failing judgement, made unsteady by his anger at having to turn for home; and it was going to get worse. We were lucky, this time. While the Myrmidons made one lightning charge after another, the cavalry formed up and circled round the Mallians, attacking them in the flank and rear. Then the infantry turned up, and the Mallians fled to their city. We followed them, struck camp outside, the siege engines trundled into position; and we were allowed to rest for the remainder of that day.

When we camp, the Spartans – my Myrmidons and Lysander's cavalry – have for a long time been sharing rations and socialising. Lysander and I joke that, when we get home, there will be many more weddings than ours. And now, that word 'home' is ringing ever more powerfully in my ears. I used to dream hardly ever, but dreaming is what I'm doing now. I get flashbacks to rides with my father and mother; to being trained in close-quarters combat by Lysander's father, Uncle Leon; and to that fateful day, when the man who stared so hard at me with my Olympic gold came to claim me and my Myrmidons. I look at the sword my father gave me, with its silver wolf head engraved on the hilt. And my heart aches with longing to see him and my mother again.

*

The Mallian citadel is a huge structure, with an inner fortress and an outer part that has a mile of walls round it. With the battering power of the catapults, it's not long before one of the gates has been forced. The siege engineers then turn their fire on the inner walls. But Alexander's patience is in short supply, and so is his better judgement. The next thing we see is him grabbing a ladder and climbing it, with only two soldiers following him – because that's all you can safely get onto a single ladder. His bodyguards frantically try to get up the remaining ladders, which collapse under their weight. They hold out their arms and call to Alexander to jump down to them. In a scene which has all the horror of a nightmare, those frightful Indian arrows whistling through the air, Alexander refuses. Over-exposed on the crest of the wall, he jumps down into the inner citadel, puts his back to the mudbrick beside a small fig tree, and begins to lay about him with his sword at his attackers, killing the Mallians' leader. For some moments, he holds his own, slashing and throwing stones. His attackers, daunted by this explosive display of bravery, fall back. Three of his bodyguards jump down to join him; one is killed instantly. Then, with the utter inevitability of Greek tragedy, Alexander falls, hit by an arrow that penetrates right through the breastplate and punctures his lung.

You may wish to skip this bit, because it is extremely bloody, as might be expected from such a serious wound. The frantic intervention of his followers saves Alexander from immediate death; they slaughter every Indian within sword distance and carry him on a shield to a tent. The arrowhead is still in the wound; an incision needs to be made to get it out. But there is already so much blood that the medics hesitate; this could kill him. In the end, his general Perdiccas comes forward and volunteers to make the incision. It is made and the arrowhead withdrawn from the wound; there is a lot more blood. For days, Alexander hovers between life and death.

The main body of the army is four days away from our location. We heard later that rumours of Alexander's death had spread like wildfire; the men were horrified, believing that he was the only one who could lead them back home. When reports reached them that he was alive and was recovering, they would not believe it. Eventually, he is placed on a boat, so that he can see his troops, and they can see him. Even then, his health is in such a fragile state that the ship is towed, rather than rowed, down the river, for fear that the slapping of the oars on the water would disturb him.

Four days later, we reach fertile countryside which has been completely deserted, so thoroughly has Alexander massacred and terrorised the native Indians; here, the king could be properly rested. Lysander told me that, once he had recovered sufficiently, Alexander was confronted by some of his close companions – probably the same men who had advised him to return. They told him that he should not expose himself so recklessly in battle. He had cheated death on that day; no large blood vessel had been touched, and the wound remained clean. But, sooner or later, his luck would run out. As it was, Alexander would suffer pain for the rest of his life from that near-fatal arrow wound; it was permanently disabling, and would make just walking, let alone fighting, an act of extreme courage. At least he took his friends' advice, and never went into battle so recklessly again.

*

After the capture of their capital city, the Mallians surrendered. Their ambassadors submitted three hundred four-horse chariots, one thousand Indian shields, a number of lions, and one hundred talents. The Oxydracians, with whom they had hoped to ally themselves, surrendered shortly afterwards.

From his sick bed, Alexander ordered the establishment of a new satrapy, which was to be ruled by a Macedonian named Peithon, and Oxyartes, the father of Roxane, his beautiful Sogdian wife. He also founded yet another Alexandria, near the confluence of the Indus and Acesines rivers. Thracian veterans and native Indians were to live here (although I bet that the Greeks would rather have gone home). Like the cities that he had already founded on a river, Nike and Bucephala, the new Alexandria was to have large dockyards. Even while he was returning, Alexander's empire-building ambitions were far from over; he still intended to develop the Indus valley.

The next opposition we had to face was from the ruler of the adjacent kingdom we had to cross, which was called Sindhu. The ruler, Musicanus, refused point blank to pay homage to Alexander, which gave our king the excuse he needed to invade. In another of the fights we like, Musicanus surrendered without a blow being exchanged, accepted the offer of a garrison, and received his new overlord in his capital city. From where Alexander immediately attacked Musicanus' neighbour, King Oxicanus. Again, this was all over quickly, and without the bloodshed that had characterised the Mallian and other previous campaigns. The next scrap on the return route was in the realm of King Sambus, whose rebellion was dispatched with similar efficiency.

Then, in April, when Alexander wanted to head for the sea, all the hard work was set at nought, when the states we had 'pacified' (military leaders like that word) revolted. Lysander told me that it was something to do with the Brahmans. At this point, Alexander lost the remaining shreds of his patience and came down on the rebels like a ton of Persian firebricks. Many were killed, the Brahmans were hanged, and the treacherous King Musicanus was crucified. King Sambus escaped. The rebellion spread to the northern regions as well, and it took some months before our various armies 'pacified' the country, which, I hear you say correctly, meant that many more people died.

When the dust of battle settled, Alexander could focus once again on how he was going to get everyone home. He decided on a three-pronged approach. One of the armies that had been sent to suppress the rebellions was commanded by the very successful general, Craterus. (As far as Alexander was concerned, Craterus was a bit too successful, so he kept sending him on honourable missions, to keep him out of the way.) Craterus commanded about a third of the army, including a number of war elephants, donated during various surrenders; after he had put down the rebellions, he was given orders to continue west, through the Bolan pass, to Carmania, and Persis. Going home route number one.

Another part of the army was to sail along the almost unknown shores of the Indian Ocean and Persian Gulf, in an exploratory as well as a homeward-bound capacity. Going home route number two.

And the remaining number – around fifty to sixty thousand, Lysander and me and our troops included – were getting the hot option. Yep, going home route number three is the Gedrosian desert for us. Now, as you know, we've done desert many times before, the death march to the River Oxus being the awful worst. I can't even guess at why Alexander is choosing to do this.

But before we set off into the inferno, he wants to claim that he's sailed the Indian Ocean. As far as we Greeks are concerned, this is the very edge of the earth; the ocean surrounds the earth, like a vast, blue mantle. So we make camp within sight of the sea while the fleet is re-fitted for the return voyage, and Alexander goes on a reconnaissance sailing trip. It must have been more pleasant than riding a horse, with his dreadfully damaged lung.

During an evening walk along the beach, Lysander and I mull over the desert decision. 'Why does he want to go the desert route? He could follow the same trajectory as Craterus, or even chance it by the sea route, surely?'

Lysander's eyes are on the far horizon. 'He knows that King Cyrus the Great, the founder of the first Persian empire, once lost a whole army in the Gedrosian desert. He also knows the risks – our scouts keep him well informed.'

'Like Erebos and his men do us. So, what's he playing at this time?'

He looks at me, and his eyes could teach the ocean how to be blue. 'It's the god thing again, isn't it, my lady? He thinks he can better Cyrus, a mere mortal, because he is the son of Zeus.'

'And Ammon. And Dionysus. With connections to Heracles, and Achilles. It goes on, doesn't it?'

'To his credit, he is planning to march in the only period of the year when a crossing is possible. The monsoon rains have made the first part of the desert accessible, and if all goes well, the army would arrive in Carmania when the harvest is ready.'

'That's a big "if"!'

He says softly, 'I'm afraid that it is.'

A livelier wave than the rest washes over our bare feet as we walk the shore. He takes my hand. I clasp his firmly, and say to him, 'There's a word for what he's doing, isn't there?'

His voice has an undercurrent of anger. 'There is, my lady.'

*

I said that the death march in Persia to the River Oxus was the worst we had, up to this point, encountered. I can tell you that the march out of India across the Gedrosian desert surpassed anything that we had to endure in Persia. It was a disaster. The blazing heat and the lack of water caused appalling casualties, especially among the poor animals; most of them died of thirst, or from the effects of the burning, sun-baked sand. Sometimes, they simply sank into loose, deep sand dunes, from which they never escaped; or they were lamed by the treacherous, uneven surfaces, and had to be butchered.

The worst part for the army was the psychological beating-up of realising, after walking all night, that water had still not been found by morning. Then the marching had to continue, with the double punishment of volcanic heat as well as raging thirst.

The terrible thing, which goes against all your instincts, is that when someone fell, from exhaustion, or thirst, or heatstroke, we were not allowed to try and keep them going. No one could stay behind to give them a helping hand or ease their pain. The orders were to get on with all possible speed; the effort to save the army as a whole had to take precedence over the suffering of individuals. It's impossible to forgive yourself for obeying orders like that.

Most of the marching was at night, and many men would fall asleep and drop in their tracks. The few who had the strength to do so followed the army when they woke up again, and got through safely; but sadly, the majority did not.

Another horror was the carnage wreaked, not by the heat but by water. We Myrmidons were camped by a small stream, fast asleep, when Lysander urgently came to wake us: 'There is going to be a flash flood – you must get away from here!' And glancing at this previously innocent-looking water, we could see that it was rapidly getting swollen and overflowing its banks, although no rain was falling here. The rain was actually falling in the mountains, where the summits, in the monsoon season, arrest the clouds passing overhead, and make them condense into heavy rainfall. In a frighteningly short time, the little stream became a raging torrent looking for prey. It drowned most of the camp followers – women, children, and all the baggage animals – and swept away the royal tent, with everything it contained.

Another deadly danger of water was the one we had faced on the way to the Oxus: of soldiers drinking so immoderately that it killed them. But at least Alexander had learned from the experience: he made his halts a couple of miles or so from water, to stop his troops drinking themselves to death, and to prevent those with no self-control from plunging right into the spring or stream and spoiling the water for others.

Then came the time when the guides admitted that they no longer knew the way; all their navigation marks had been obliterated by the blown and drifting sand. There was nothing in this vast and featureless desert to determine what course they should take: no trees by the roadside, no hills of solid earth rising from the sand. The guides had never practised the art of finding their direction by the stars at night and by the sun in the daytime, unlike Phoenician sailors, who set their course by the Little Bear constellation, and the rest of us, who steer by the Great Bear.

Alexander took the matter into his own hands. Remembering how good Peg was during the three hundred-mile trek across the Sahara, he summoned Lysander and me to accompany him, and told me to give my horse his head. Peg quickly scented water, and on the same day, we found the sea. No sooner were we on the beach than Peg started scraping at the sand with his hoof. Lysander and I shovelled away the shingle – and found the godsend of fresh, clear water. The whole army soon followed, and for seven days we marched along the coast, getting our water from the beach. Finally, the guides regained their bearings and were able to set a course for the interior again.

*

THE RETURN

Hubris is the word that Lysander and I were referring to during our walk on the beach before we set off on this Hades of a journey. Hubris is the ultimate form of insolence or defiance to the gods. Or to any other authority to whom you may be answerable.

It wasn't necessary for us to march through the Gedrosian desert for sixty days. Just as it wasn't necessary for us to invade India. Alexander should have acknowledged that India was too powerful for him. With its lethal archers, thousands of war elephants, and proud and mighty chieftains and warriors. With its god-like rivers, so deep and wide and fast. And with its climate, that could lay us low with terrible deserts and drown us with torrential rain.

In not bowing to a power far mightier than he was, Alexander nearly lost his life, and he sacrificed countless thousands of others. If he had just stopped once he had Persia under his belt, things would have been very different. And he might have lived a lot longer. But I don't think that a long life was ever what Alexander wanted. All he wanted was to be the second Achilles. Yet, paradoxically, he achieved a great deal more than his hero.

ELEVEN

WEDDINGS AT SUSA

When we finally reached the city of Pura, in Persia, it was early December and the winter rains were starting. Alexander had dispatched messengers to the satrap of Drangiana, north of Pura and one of the most fertile areas, and they had sent food. This touches on an aspect of Alexander's leadership which places him well above anything that his hero, Achilles, could ever have achieved. Because Alexander completely redefined how wars can be fought in the way that he organised and sustained his army. The Gedrosian desert was his one, awful mistake; the rest, it has to be said, was sheer brilliance.

Like Uncle Leon told me, in our briefing session before Lysander and I set off, Alexander owed much to his father, King Philip the Second of Macedon. It was Philip's reforms to the logistics of how armies should be run that provided his son Alexander with the most efficient supply system ever.

WEDDINGS AT SUSA

Previously, battles consisted of one Greek city-state fighting another. They would leave their home city and travel very slowly to an agreed battleground, suitable for phalanx warfare. Travel was slow, because they had thousands of non-combatants tagging along: attendants, women, children and slaves. Often, there were more taggers-along than actual troops. Consequently, tons of ox-drawn wagonloads of food were needed to feed everyone. These armies would engage their enemy in one decisive battle and then go home. Again, very slowly.

Philip made sweeping reforms to all this. And he had a wonderful precedent in the Athenian commander, Xenophon (under whom my father and Uncle Leon had the honour of serving when they repelled the most recent Persian invasion). To lead his Ten Thousand home after the would-be king of Persia, Cyrus, got himself killed, the first thing Xenophon did was burn the ox-drawn carts, significantly increasing speed and general mobility. Philip followed up on this example by making horses his main pack animal, and, as Penelope noticed when we set off for Persia, each soldier carries his own supplies, including arms, armour, road-building tools, blankets, medical supplies, and up to a month's supply of flour, in a backpack. A total weight of around eighty pounds.

Philip also kicked out all the non-combatants. At first, so did Alexander. But when it became clear that his men would not see their families again for years, he began to relax the rules a bit, allowing them to marry captured women. But he still kept his army travelling as light and as fast as possible.

While horses and mules were Alexander's main transport animals in the early parts of the campaign, from Egypt onwards, camels became indispensable. A horse or a mule can carry two hundred pounds over a long distance; a camel can carry three hundred pounds. They were also perfect for crossing arid terrain, with few limitations on what they could eat or drink. Throughout his campaigns, horses, mules, and camels remained the engines of his baggage train. Their speed and endurance were far greater than oxen, and well suited to the light, fast marches across harsh terrain that brought him victory, time and time again.

He still had to use carts to transport the really heavy items, such as siege machinery and the wounded. And when he hit inland Asia, hotly pursuing Darius, he had to confront a logistical problem that no military commander had ever faced before. He was many miles away from his base in Macedonia. There was the constant threat of banditry. And, in the largely arid east, he could not count on a ready food supply. This is where Alexander's genius outshone anything that his hero Achilles could ever have done.

It goes like this. Having crushed the Persian king, Darius, in two major battles, at Issus and Gaugamela, Alexander had by then a glittering and fearful reputation. Persian officials surrendered to him in great numbers, well before he reached their territory. And Alexander realised that this was his quick fix to supply problems. He sent messengers ahead of his army to meet the officials, to secure arrangements for the army's supply through their territory. On some occasions, he took hostages to ensure that the officials stuck to their side of the bargain.

WEDDINGS AT SUSA

Where local officials did not surrender to Alexander, he took a different approach. He would inform himself in detail about the region – the topography, routes, climate, and resources – before deciding on his next move. Then, he would either launch a lightning campaign against the region, with a small, elite force, while the rest of the army remained behind in a safe, well-resourced base. Or, he would split his forces into smaller units that would gain supplies, either by sacking settlements or by foraging.

The one time this incredibly effective strategy failed was the Gedrosian desert. It was the greatest logistical error of Alexander's life. Lysander told me later that Alexander was expecting his army to be supplied by the navy, commanded by his admiral Nearchus, as it made its way along the coast. But monsoon winds delayed the fleet from leaving India for months. So seventy-five per cent of the army that set out onto those deadly wastes – mostly the baggage train – withered and perished.

The Gedrosian desert was the one exception. Alexander was a leader who cared so much about feeding and supplying his army that he put endless creative thought into it. He had organised a permanent supply line of my three-barbed arrows to be transported from the forges of Sparta into Macedon, and from there across Persia to wherever we were. Fresh horses came from Danae's stud, too: vital, when some of the Myrmidons lost their beloved four-legged friends. On several occasions, he sent home many hundreds of men who were too old or too ill for service, arranging for reinforcements, recruited from Macedon and Greece, to take their place. No one before him had run a vast army in the field so far from its home, and for so long. Everything Alexander did was a first; he was so much more than a (frequently reckless) hero in battle, and an inspirational leader – he was a brilliant strategist and organiser.

*

When we reached Pura, roughly four hundred miles from Persepolis, the Alexander organising machine had clicked back into gear, and there was food and drink galore. In fact, such was the mood after all the dreadful hardship that it turned into a seven-day, travelling, completely wild party. Alexander, who numbered the god of ecstasy, Dionysus, among the many in his extensive family tree, gave orders for the villages along his route to be strewn with flowers and garlands, and for bowls full of wine to be set out on the thresholds of houses. He had wagons covered in planks and rigged out like tents, with expensive textiles so that soldiers could party in groups. He himself, with his Companion Cavalry and elite commanders, went in front, their heads wreathed with flowers woven into garlands, riding in wagons weighed down with golden bowls and huge gold goblets.

For the Spartan contingent in Alexander's army, this really was not our thing. In Sparta, it's considered shameful, stupid, and dangerous to be drunk. And before you groan 'party poopers!', think about it. At any time during that weaving, double-visioned, brain-dead carouse, a half-competent rebel horde could have swooped and taken out thousands of soldiers without anyone even knowing what was happening. Plus, the after-effects of drinking such vast quantities of unwatered wine can be not just painful and pitiful but lethal. If you consider how many have died in this campaign simply from consuming too much water, too fast, it's no stretch of the imagination to picture what too much wine can do.

When the partying was over, it was quite possibly because Alexander was still suffering from the mother of all hangovers that he came down so harshly on the offenders, when he was faced with a long and bitter string of complaints from the Persians over whom he had appointed his satraps. It appeared that, during his absence, many of his officials had used their new powers arbitrarily and selfishly, and had committed serious offences. Others were accused of sacrilege, which is certainly plausible, as we've already seen how little the Greeks and Macedonians understood Zoroastrianism, including Alexander himself, with his insulting images on the coins he minted.

Alexander had to show the Persians that he took their complaints seriously. Many offenders he replaced; others were imprisoned; some were executed. Alexander also wrote to all his generals and satraps in Asia, ordering them to disband all their mercenaries with immediate effect and send them to him. This was a highly useful move, as he had left many thousands of Greeks behind in the new towns in the east and lost many more thousands in the Gedrosian desert. It also, of course, reduced the satraps' capacity to obstruct his orders.

These administrative measures were taken while Alexander was resting the army and himself in a coastal city called Salmous, awaiting the arrival of his fleet under Admiral Nearchus. The fleet, the late departure of which from India had precipitated the Gedrosian desert disaster, had been ordered to return by way of the Indian Ocean and to explore the coastal waters. Alexander was holding a dramatic contest in the theatre, with his elite officers and Spartan troops invited to join the audience. Sitting with Lysander, I am marvelling at the experience of being presented with an entertainment other than warfare, when the fleet sails into the harbour. Nearchus makes a dramatic entrance into the theatre, and the entire audience greets the safe return of the ships with tumultuous applause.

Many and wonderful were the tales the mariners had to tell. They told of wildly dangerous currents, and numerous large and unexpected islands. But their most extraordinary experience was an encounter with a large school of simply enormous whales. The sailors were understandably terrified and despaired of their lives, thinking that they would be dashed to pieces by a mere flip of the tail of one of these juggernauts. But when they all shouted in unison, and blew trumpets, and beat their shields to make a huge racket, the whales were alarmed by the noise, and plunged into the depths of the sea.

Walking along the beach with Lysander afterwards, watching the curling waves lapping over our feet, I reach for his hand. He squeezes mine more tightly than usual. And I know that he has something to tell me. The last time we walked along a beach, it was just before the terrible trek across the Gedrosian desert. Now, I simply feel grateful that we and our loyal troops are still alive. But that word 'home' is echoing again in my ears, as is my namesake's flying horse song, being sung by my father. Yet, my instincts are saying that Lysander does not have good news to give me.

Looking towards the horizon, where the sun is doing a good imitation of Hephaestos' forge fire, he says, 'At a meeting of the generals yesterday, Alexander said he plans to proceed to Susa, where he will marry Stateira, the elder daughter of Darius. He will give her younger sister, Drypetis, as wife to Hephaestion.'

'More marriages of political convenience? To cement his kingship?'

'Yes.' But Lysander is not sounding like himself.

My stomach tightens as I say, 'Well, at least we're still travelling in the homewards direction. Susa is only two hundred miles from Babylon.'

There is a long pause before Lysander says, as the pace of our walk slows, 'That is not all. Alexander wishes the most prominent of his friends and elite officers to take wives also. He wishes to give to them in marriage the noblest Persian princesses, who, for some time now, have been benefiting from a Greek education.'

I stop us both, turn him to me, and take his other hand. 'You're sounding like the Big A's public-relations oracle! Level with me, Lysander! He wants to tie you into one of these forced marriages, doesn't he?'

The way he looks at me breaks my heart; his own must be breaking too. He whispers, 'We can't run home to Sparta. Too many consequences.'

'We can't run anywhere. But I will always love you. And I know that you will always love me.'

At last, he smiles, becoming himself again. He whispers, 'Trust me. I will find a way.'

'I do trust you.' I slip into his arms, as the sun sinks, and Hephaestos' forge turns to a smouldering crimson.

*

I'm woken early the next morning, shaken gently awake by Hephaestion. I know him quite well, now, after Lysander's and my ventures with him and Alexander, pursuing mythological and deity-related connections. Hephaestion is actually one of the loveliest men I've ever met. He has a very beautiful and gentle face, although he also has a tremendous reputation as a senior commander. I have a huge respect for this man whom Alexander loves, like Achilles loved Patroclus. He whispers, 'Might you be in a frame of mind to breakfast with you-know-who?'

I lift myself onto one elbow. 'Depends on what's for breakfast.'

'He says that's up to you.'

'Give me a clue!'

He smiles and shakes his head.

'Well, give me five minutes to stink a bit less!'

Breakfast with Alexander is not something I've done before. But, in view of what Lysander told me last night, I'm not altogether surprised. Ninety-eight per cent of me is burning with anger at what he has done to us. The remaining two per cent is curious as to what he will do next. He must be getting really bored, with no wars left to fight.

As I reach his tent, I can see that it's recently had a makeover. The fabrics, which took a beating in the big on-road party, have been replaced with choice silks and golden braids. Eastern rugs adorn the floor, which my naked, toughened feet, now even more blasted by the Gedrosian desert, don't even notice.

He's sitting on a Persian-style throne to receive me: gold-adorned, with jewelled inlays. He probably nicked it from Darius. I'll bet that Darius' bath is not far away, either. He's wearing a purple, Persian-style cloak, with gold neck clasps. I'm in my usual Spartan army crimson. Crimson is a good colour for a fighter; when Lysander took over from the fallen Admetus, no one could see the blood that was pouring from his shoulder, until he himself fell.

I salute my leader, seeing again those hungry eyes that have brought me and my Myrmidons, and Lysander and his faithful cavalry, all this way. Looking at that face, I can see that not much has changed over the years. He has scars where he did not when he confronted my father and Lysander's in Sparta. A deep slash across the forehead, and another at the side of his neck. And he has a scar in his lung that will slow him for the rest of his life. But he is still a very handsome, powerful man. I, too, have picked up a few scars – mostly minor flesh wounds, thanks to Spartan armour and the P-to-W. But I know that I am no longer at my strongest, after that deadly fever.

At my salute, he stands and dismisses his bodyguards; then, he motions me to his side. His damaged lung must make any movement painful. Feeling intensely sorry for him, I go right up to him. 'Sir, what can I do to help you?'

The shake of the head is the usual dismissive Alexander. His breathing carries the rasp of the damaged lung. 'Rather, this is about what I can do to help you, Princess Lydia. I wish you to do me the honour of becoming my wife.'

My surprise is entirely feigned; I was expecting this. 'I… I am greatly honoured myself, sir. But… you already have a wife. And intend to take a second.'

'As the King of Kings, I can bestow that honour on as many women as I wish.'

I don't think about this response at all; it just leaps from my lips. 'Not where I come from, sir!' (Actually, this is not strictly true. Lycurgus, Sparta's legendary law-giver, said that an older man married to a young wife could ask a suitable younger man to father his children, if he felt that this would produce stronger offspring. However, marriages in Sparta are still generally monogamous.)

The rasp is there again, as Alexander replies, 'Ah, yes. The troublesome Sparta once more.'

And again, I open my big mouth. 'The troublesome Spartans who have been putting their lives on the line for you, for years now, sir.'

He comes very close to me; I don't move. 'I could force you to accept this honour. You know that, don't you?'

'You could try.' I am quite proud of myself for this Laconian reply.

There is a pause, during which I brace myself for an explosion of anger. Then, he relaxes, backing off, with a smile and a slight bow. 'Princess Lydia of Sparta, you are an admirable adversary! I would not wish to face you in battle.'

'And I wish to continue as adversary to your enemies, sir. That is the way I can best serve you. But I thank you from my heart for your offer; it does me great honour.' Saluting the King of Kings, I leave his lavish tent, annoyed to find myself shaking slightly as I make my way back to the Myrmidons' camp. I do not go alone; ever the gentleman, Hephaestion kindly walks at my side.

*

Lysander and I ride with Alexander and Hephaestion one last time to be the king's 'eloquent witnesses'. On the way to Susa, our leader leaves the army to rest, while we four make our way to Pasargadae. This time, Hephaestion has arranged for Alexander to ride in a horse-drawn wagon, to try and make him more comfortable, although it must still be a gruelling journey. But he is driven by his wish to be crowned King of Kings in the Persian tradition, near the tomb of Cyrus the Great, the ancient founder of the first Persian empire. When he last visited Pasargadae, this was not possible, because Darius was still alive. Unfortunately, it is still not possible, because when we get there, we find that the tomb has been desecrated. It has been broken into by grave robbers; Cyrus' body has been thrown to the floor, and many precious things have been stolen. For a long time, Alexander stares at the scene of destruction, saying nothing. Hephaestion stands close at his side.

Looking at the devastation, Lysander whispers to me, 'I have never seen him look so shocked. This is greatly affecting him.'

Hugely comforted by having my lover with me again, even if not for very long, I reply, 'It *is* shocking. I wonder if he sees it as a portent.'

On the way back, Alexander's closest friend rides in the wagon with him, while I tell Lysander about the king's proposal of marriage. He says quietly, 'It was brave of you to refuse, when I did not.'

'You *could not*! He would have had you executed for insubordination!'

Lysander is silent for a few minutes. Then, he says, 'Alexander has sent for Damon, to lead my cavalry back to Sparta from Susa. I have been in touch with Erebos; the Krypteia will provide an undercover escort for you all and keep a line of communication open.'

And now the reality hits, like one of my own triple-barbed arrows, straight into the heart. Everyone is going home, except for him. 'Do we have to watch the wedding ceremonies before we leave?'

His voice is slightly unsteady. 'I am very sorry, my lady, but that is Alexander's plan.'

I bite my lip so hard that I can taste blood.

*

Alexander gave orders for the tomb to be restored, and the army continued to Persepolis and, finally, Susa. Here, the preparations for many festivities were in full swing. The navy had made its way from Salmous around the coast, so army and navy were re-united. Many valiant soldiers and officers were decorated, including, as Alexander had promised at

WEDDINGS AT SUSA

Tyre, Lysander, for leading the men of the fallen Admetus in their charge into the citadel. To my astonishment, as Lysander descends from the podium, my name is called. As I mount the steps, Lysander and I pass so close to each other, I can feel the warmth of his body; I will never forget the love in his eyes.

On the podium, waiting for me with a golden crown, is the gentle Hephaestion. Beyond him, on his bejewelled throne, Alexander looks on with a slight smile. 'We owe the victory at the Persian Gate to you and your Myrmidons. Never let it be said that Alexander was ungrateful for your prowess.' Never, indeed. Just take away the man I love, and make him marry a Persian instead of a Spartan princess.

The greatest of the festivities was, of course, the marriage ceremony, which lasted five days. Dancers, actors, and musicians had come all the way from Greece to add glamour to the event. And it turned out that Alexander was marrying not one but two Persian princesses from different dynastic lines. In addition to Stateira, eldest daughter of Darius, he was also tying the knot with Parysatis, a daughter of Darius' predecessor. Quite what Roxane, his beautiful Sogdian first wife, thought about this, only became evident a while later.

I expect you can easily recall the worst moment in your life so far. For me, it was looking at Lysander standing with an undeniably beautiful Persian princess called Calliope, while they were showered with flowers and dried fruits. But even this acutely painful experience was tempered by two things. Firstly, Calliope looked anything but happy. I suddenly thought, she doesn't want this any more than Lysander and I do. What suitor have they torn her away from? And I began to feel sorrier for her than I did for myself. The second thing that got me through this was realising that Damon had arrived from Sparta and was standing at my side.

The next day, excused from having to endure further weddings, Damon and I set off with Lysander's cavalry and my Myrmidons. As the dust blows from under the hooves of our horses, into a cloud stretching back down the road towards the city of Susa, this tight feeling in my chest gets steadily worse until I can hardly breathe. Sensing my misery, Pegasus walks more and more slowly. Damon turns to me, reaches across, and touches my arm. 'You must trust him, Liddy. To mourn him like this is almost giving up on him, isn't it?'

'That's what he said. That I must trust him.'

'You must. Because he will never give up on you.'

That night, I dream about when Lysander and I were talking about regicides, over our campfire. Then, he got up, saying we had to check the horses. And something snapped inside me at the thought of parting for the night. And I said, hugging him tightly, '*When we get back to Sparta, will you marry me? Because I think I might die, if you don't!*' Then, I wake. The campfire embers are glowing dully. Peg is grazing peacefully, next to Lysander's horse, Hector, who is coming back to Sparta with us. Damon is camped with Lysander's cavalry. And I think to myself, 'You haven't left all of Lysander behind. You have quite a lot of him, right here by your side. So you'd better not die, had you?'

*

WEDDINGS AT SUSA

All through those thousands of miles homewards, Damon asks me to tell him everything about Lysander and me. And it is an immense comfort to talk about the man I love. It must be good for Damon, too, knowing what I know now, about the love he bears his brother.

During the journey, we get regular updates from Krypteian agents about Alexander's movements. On the approach to Babylon, as the high walls rise ahead of us, Damon spends some time talking with a Krypteian who has arrived on a lathered horse.

We camp that night outside the walls, looking up at shooting stars. And I remember that my father must have done the same, when he went to sue for peace from the King of Kings, in vain. Instead, the largest Persian invasion ever threatened all Greece, an invasion that my father and uncle took on and won, with a united Sparta and Athens.

Uniting nations is far from easy, as Alexander is finding out. Damon thoughtfully stirs the flames of the campfire. 'It would seem that the forced marriages have worsened relations between Alexander and his Macedonian high command. Apparently, he made a number of Macedonian bridegrooms wear purple dresses, in the Persian tradition.'

'At least he didn't subject Lysander to that!'

Damon smiles. 'Indeed. But he really does seem to be going native, which is outraging his own people, and the Macedonian troops as a whole. The rank and file feel utterly humiliated and rejected, to have fought so hard against Persia only to see a new, strong Persian king in the end.'

'We lost so many of the Companion Cavalry in the

Gedrosian desert that he had to hire Persian horsemen to replace them.'

'And our informant has told me that much worse is happening: a regiment of thirty thousand young Bactrians has arrived in Susa. They have been trained to fight in the phalanx and are called the Epigonoi – the "successors".'

'Alexander has never understood what tact is.' I tell Damon about the appalling designs on the coins he had minted, that were so sacrilegious to the Persians. 'He's always upset everyone and pleased no one.'

'I'm afraid it gets worse still. Some Macedonian soldiers have been throwing insults, such as, "Fight your wars with your father, Ammon!", and it sounds like the criticism is correct.'

'Ever since he killed Cleitus the Black in a drunken rage, he will only accept flattery.'

Damon adds, 'He's had thirteen soldiers executed for insubordination and dismissed his European soldiers.'

'Confirming their worst fears, that he's building a Persian army! He's playing a dangerous game, driving his own army to mutiny.'

Damon gets up to check the horses. 'My informant tells me that the soldiers apologised in the end, and he smoothed things over with a large banquet.'

I get up to go with him. 'I'll bet that was Hephaestion's idea. Whatever would Alexander do without him?' The next news that arrives makes my final comment prophetic, in a very sad way.

*

The satrap of Babylonia, Mazaeus, allows us to take our troops through Babylon, with the cavalry dismounted and leading their animals. Our march then takes us towards the lush deltas of the Tigris and the Euphrates, into the land called Mesopotamia – 'land between rivers'. On the way, we pass not far from the battlefield of Gaugamela, and I describe to Damon how Lysander and I agreed that this was absolutely the finest battle of Alexander's campaign. His blue-grey eyes follow my story intently, and he smiles with delight when I explain how the phalanx opened so neatly to foil the scythed chariots of Darius.

We camp that night in some woods, where there is excellent grazing for the horses. And it is while Damon and I are taking some food that a Krypteian scout arrives with the news: Hephaestion is dead. I stare at him in disbelief. 'He... he can't be!'

'I am very sorry, my lady, to be the bearer of such sad tidings. It has greatly affected the king.'

Damon gives the man a flask of water and leads his horse to a stream to drink. I motion the Krypteian to sit down and help himself to food. 'What happened?'

'Alexander had gone to Ecbatana in Media, with Hephaestion, where they were entertained by the satrap of that country, who is a man called Atropates. After an evening of feasting and drinking, Hephaestion was taken ill. Seven days later, he died.'

'Could he have been poisoned?'

'Alexander must believe so. He ordered the execution of Hephaestion's doctor.'

'He must be devastated.'

'He fasted for three days. He cut his hair and ordered the tails of the military horses to be clipped. We heard that he also sent an embassy to the oracle at Siwa in Egypt, to ask Zeus Ammon what kind of burial he wanted Hephaestion to have.'

The next day, when we're on the move again, Damon rides up to take his usual place beside me. 'I'm afraid that Alexander has got himself into some serious trouble. I just hope, in a way, that no one explains it to him.'

'What do you mean, Damon?'

'He has proclaimed to all the peoples of Asia that they should quench what the Persians call the sacred fire until such time as Hephaestion's funeral is ended.'

'What is he thinking about? The Zoroastrian custom is to quench the fire at the death of the king!'

Damon nods in assent. Then he says what I'm thinking. 'What Alexander has in fact announced is his own death.'

*

Winter has arrived when we get to Cilicia, with the arid deserts of Gedrosia and Bactria now many hundreds of miles behind us. I've read about these lands in Xenophon's account of the Ten Thousand's march towards Babylon. So many times, that I can quote it to Damon: *'large and beautiful plain country, well-watered and thickly covered with trees of all sorts and vines. Shut in on all sides by a steep and lofty wall of mountains from sea to sea'*. We stop to let the horses drink and wade in a shallow river, and I gaze at the mountains, their peaks wreathed in clouds. To think that my father, and Lysander and Damon's father, have come this way, brings home suddenly closer.

Passing the site of the battle of Issus, I give Damon the highlights. He winces when I tell him about the Persians' brutality to our sick and injured men. And shakes his head at the Persians' disastrous choice of position, penned in by water and mountains on all sides. Then I tell him about Lysander's courage at Tyre, leading the charge into the citadel, after Admetus fell. Damon smiles. 'Brave little brother.'

'By how much are you the elder brother?'

'By two hours. Our mother used to tease Lysander that he was giving her problems even before he was born!'

'Was he a mischief-maker?'

'He used to wind me up a lot.' Damon's blue-grey eyes look directly into mine. 'But his attachment to you began from a very tender age. He saw every male as a rival.'

I remember the hungry look in the boy Lysander's eyes, that I was too young to understand. Damon must have seen my expression change, because he says softly, 'You have made him very much happier than he was for a long time, Liddy. And you must trust him – remember?'

'This leaving him is so hard!'

'You can now help him by being where he will come to find you. Sparta.'

That evening, we receive news that Alexander has gone to Babylonia. And the Greek world has received orders, firstly, that all exiles have to return home. Damon comments, 'He may be the leader of the Corinthian League, but it is questionable whether he is entitled to do this.'

'It's bound to cause trouble to flare up. And that'll give him an excuse to intervene and tighten his grip on the Greek towns.'

Damon says grimly, 'So the next time we're invaded, it'll be by a Macedonian king at the head of a Persian army!'

The second edict that Alexander issues to the Greeks is that they must worship him as a god. Damon, who has read his history, says, 'It's an unusual request but not unheard of. Alexander's father, Philip, once ordered his own throne to be placed between statues of the twelve Olympian gods. And several Greek commanders have received sacrifices.'

'Deification is something Alexander has been angling for throughout his campaign!' I tell Damon about the visits to Troy and Gordium in Persia, Siwa in Egypt, and Nysa in India, where Lysander and I were supposed to be Alexander's 'eloquent witnesses'.

Damon looks thoughtful. 'There have been examples where humans could be more powerful than the gods. Such as when prayers to the gods didn't end a famine, but the help of a king did.'

'And there are many myths about mortals who became gods – like Heracles. My father's watchword in attacking the Persians was "Zeus, Saviour; Heracles, Leader!"'

Damon smiles. 'It sounds like you and my brother had more than a little sympathy for Alexander's deification aspirations!'

'That's the maddening thing about Alexander. He can do – he has done – things that tear you apart. But he can still make you want to follow him to the ends of the earth.'

Damon smiles again, looking and sounding more like

his twin than ever. 'Sometimes you call it hubris, sometimes charisma. Yes?'

'Yes.'

Alexander's request was taken seriously by most cities, although not by Sparta, where the ephors decreed ironically: 'Since Alexander wishes to be a god, let him be a god.' But the move did alienate the Greeks even more from the man who had already caused huge tensions, by ordering the return of the exiles. He had offended his soldiers; he had created troubles in Greece. And he had lost his best friend. He must have been becoming very lonely. I wondered bitterly how Lysander was getting on with his new wife.

*

With Cilicia two hundred miles behind us, we reach Troy. And this is where we will no longer be retracing Alexander's steps, because we will not be crossing the Hellespont, and going home via Macedonia. We will be retracing the voyage of my father and Uncle Leon, when they went with their elite early strike force, from Sparta direct to Troy. At Damon's orders, a fleet of Spartan triremes awaits us at Troy. But Poseidon is, as my father says, 'in a grumpy mood'; heavy storm clouds are streaking the skies, and the Aegean is chucking angry grey waves at the shore. The triremes are pulled up safely on the beach in a nearby cove. In the evening, their admiral comes to our camp to greet us, and Damon's smile is his sunniest as he brings this strong, dark-tanned commander to meet me. 'Liddy, this is my namesake, the admiral of our little fleet – I am so happy to introduce you!'

I AM LYDIA

The admiral bows, but I am still in my army uniform, and I hold out my hand to greet this man who played such a large part in the last Persian defeat. 'My cousin has a great deal to live up to in you, sir.'

He takes my hand in a powerful grasp, as if I were a man rather than a woman; I like that. 'Your father has told me that you are setting the name of Lydia among the stars, Commander.'

'I didn't know that my father was a poet as well as a warrior!'

'Your father – and this young warrior's father – are the finest kings that Sparta has ever gloried in, Commander.'

Damon laughs, steering the naval commander to a place by the campfire, where food and water wait. 'Only because they have the best of admirals, sir! Now, tell us – how long before we can safely set sail?'

While we wait for the storm clouds and the gales to subside, more news is received. Alexander is facing difficulties as to how he should enter Babylon, where he wishes to set up his court. When he and his men arrived outside the high walls, an astrologer and soothsayer of the Esagila temple complex, called Belephantes, came to Alexander, saying that he should not enter the town through the eastern gate. This was because he would have to enter facing west, where the sun goes down, and the sun is the symbol of the Macedonian royal house. So this astrologer was being very thoughtful and careful in not wanting to create bad omens on the king's entry into the city called the Gate of the Gods.

Apparently, Alexander took this very seriously and tried to march his army through the Royal Gate, where he would be facing east as he entered Babylon, but it would appear that the swampy terrain made this impossible. I can't understand his problem. 'When my father and Philemon entered Babylon, it was through the Ishtar Gate. They would have been coming from the west, facing east. Why couldn't Alexander just make the march round the city to the Ishtar Gate?'

Damon says, 'I don't think that we have the whole story here. There could have been other reasons why the Royal Gate wasn't an option.'

This is so like talking to his very rational and thoughtful brother that it's uncanny. 'Go on.'

Damon looks at me with those calm, blue-grey eyes. 'Alexander still hasn't been crowned king, has he? So, technically at least, and maybe religiously as well, he has no right to enter through the Royal Gate.'

And now, I'm thinking back. 'He tried twice to get crowned king at Cyrus' tomb in Pasargadae. The first time, he couldn't, because Darius was still alive. The second time, the tomb had been desecrated.'

Damon's voice continues at its quiet, measured rate, so like his brother's. 'And the fact that he's still *behaving* like a king – or an autocrat, or a tyrant, and has the power to enforce his will – doesn't mean that he can enter Babylon as a king.'

'So, he has to enter facing west.'

'The wrong direction. After already having announced his own death, by ordering the Persians' sacred fire to be quenched.'

I AM LYDIA

*

The winds settle, and all looks set fair for the voyage to Sparta. The triremes are lined up on the beach, and Peg positively herds the cavalry's horses on board – he knows exactly where we're going. The Myrmidons and Lysander's cavalry are now so mixed together in chatting, laughing groups that Damon and I haven't the heart to enforce discipline – after all, don't they deserve a holiday cruise?

The voyage back to Sparta takes seven days and nights, the same time it took my father, and Damon and Lysander's, to sail to Troy on their epic pre-emptive-strike mission. As he was with our warrior fathers, Poseidon is kind. The waves are still high and the wind strong; but it is blowing us homewards to Sparta. The Aegean is lapis lazuli blue, and flying fish escort us on our way. Shortly after we've pushed off from the shore, a massive wave of sleep engulfs me, as though it's the first time I can really relax in years. And for once, I don't dream; whereas recently, all my dreams have been full of the family I am missing so sorely.

When I wake, my head is on Damon's shoulder and his arm is round me, to cushion me from the pitching and rolling of an increasingly rough sea. Struggling up, I rush to the side and am violently sick; I have discovered that I am no sailor. I might have survived the crossing of the Hellespont, where the sea was mirror calm. But these boisterous waves are more than I can take. Damon gently wipes my face, like a kindly big brother.

Even during the seven-day voyage, the information machine of the Krypteia keeps ticking over. We get news

WEDDINGS AT SUSA

that, after Alexander had to enter Babylon through the wrong gate, numerous embassies came to do homage to the conqueror and discuss politics. And they brought many complaints, especially the Greek towns, which had been forced to take back troublesome exiles, including thousands of wandering mercenaries and political rebels.

We only found out after getting back to Sparta that Alexander had been dreaming up another war, this time against the Arabs, who had not yet recognised him as king. Alexander's Admiral Nearchus had proved that it was possible to ship large armies to distant countries; a substantial navy had been prepared to transport the expeditionary force, and reconnaissance operations had been carried out far and wide. Alexander was planning to sail through the Red Sea until he was in Egypt.

But the conquest of Arabia was just the beginning of Alexander's new vision. From Egypt, and with a new, even larger fleet, built in Cilicia, he wanted to attack Carthage, Sicily, and Italy. These were not unrealistic plans; Carthage at this time was very weak.

Alexander also ordered the speeding-up of repairs to the Esagila temple complex, which he had promised when he first entered Babylon as conqueror. This huge and magnificent temple had been damaged hundreds of years before by the Persian king, Xerxes, after a Babylonian revolt. And it is from this temple that the soothsayer Belephantes came, with his warnings about entering Babylon through the wrong gate. So Alexander must have been wondering about who he should listen to. At this point, he really was on his own.

And something inside me wanted to go to him and help him. All through that voyage from Troy to Sparta, these invisible cords tugged at my heart. I yearned to return to where Alexander was. But only because that was where I might find Lysander.

*

In the end, Alexander took the advice of Greek philosophers, who argued that perhaps the astrologers did not wish him to see the Esagila temple because the funds he had made available had been misappropriated. So he entered Babylon through the fateful westward-facing gate. In the event, it was clear that the funding excuse was a complete fabrication, because work on the temple was well advanced.

However, the astrologers of Babylon were still deeply afraid that something would happen to Alexander. So they organised a ritual to try and avert the danger. It was based on the Persian belief that, if an evil omen threatened the king, a substitute king could be appointed. If this substitute king sat on the throne, evil would hurt him, and the real king would remain safe. So, one hot day when Alexander was away from his throne to inspect his troops, a person of humble origin went to the throne. The eunuchs who guarded the throne let this person pass, because they understood what was going on. As soon as the man sat on the throne, they started to show all signs of mourning, and did nothing to remove him. Nothing happened to him either, so the eunuchs can hardly have concluded that their attempt to protect the king had been successful. Even if

Alexander had known about this event, he would not have understood it.

A few days after this ritual, the embassy that Alexander had sent to Siwa returned. The oracle had considered Alexander's question about how Hephaestion's funeral should be conducted. Zeus Ammon permitted Alexander's beloved friend to be venerated as a demi-god – *heros*. This news had to be celebrated with the usual drinking party. And there were other reasons to be cheerful: in a few days, the expeditionary force would leave for Arabia, and Alexander would have been looking forward to the first addition to his empire in more than two years.

TWELVE

'DOOMED TO LIVE BUT FOR A LITTLE SEASON'
Achilles, The *Iliad*, Book 1

As the shores of my beloved Laconia come into view, it's not sea spray that almost blinds me. Standing next to me at the prow of the leaping ship, Damon puts a comforting arm around my shoulders. He knows exactly what is going through my head and filling my heart. But, when we make shore, and my father's arms are around me, even Damon does not know what news has arrived by carrier pigeon, from the Krypteia in Babylon. 'Prepare yourself for this, Liddy. Alexander is dead.'

The sand beneath my feet seems to shift, and I stagger to keep my balance. 'No, that can't be right! It's Hephaestion who is dead!'

My father's strong arms hold me up as he walks me to where Pegasus is waiting. 'I am so sorry, Liddy. The day after a drinking party, to celebrate the news about Hephaestion's funeral, Alexander woke up very ill. Ten days later, he died.'

The following days are full of grief for Alexander. When you have fought for someone who has been your leader for so long, he occupies a huge place in your heart. Alexander had torn the man I loved away from me, breaking two hearts. But this giant of a man had been such a dominant part of my life, and Lysander's life, for such a long and intense period, that I was engulfed in sorrow for him. I found that I could not eat, and even drinking was difficult.

In the end, it was Damon who brought me back from this brink. He takes me out for a ride, me on Peg and he on Lysander's Hector. We go to the foothills of Mount Taygetos where, all that time ago, we Myrmidons had proved ourselves worthy of joining the Spartan army. The cavalry assault course is still there. And Damon says, casually, 'Did your father ever show you where you were found as a baby on this mountain?'

'No. But I'm sure he would do if I asked.'

'Of course he would. In fact, it was Lysander who asked our father to show him where you were found. We were eight years old, and father had just told us about where you had come from.'

'I was seven when my father told me that I was found abandoned on the mountain. So it must have been around the same time.'

'Lysander was so head over heels in love with you, even aged eight, that he wanted to know all about you. So my father took both of us up the mountain, to the place where the Krypteia had found a very small, cold, and hungry baby girl.'

I have to smile. 'That's never changed. My mother tells me I was always hungry!'

'My father was coming down the mountain to fetch your mother and father when he encountered them. They had just had the tragic news about your namesake. Something drove them up the mountain.' He dismounts. 'It gets quite steep, so we'll leave our horses here.'

As we climb steadily, I remember something. 'My parents used to mind sheep when they were teenagers. Father told me that they used to lure a big wolf to the sheep in the next valley, to protect their own. They were quite often on the mountain at night.'

'And that's how my father first met yours, and your mother.'

'Father said he was certain at first that the Krypteia were going to execute the pair of them for breaking the curfew!'

'And my father told them, "You are behind the times. We are recruiting, not executing, now."'

'That's word for word what my father has told me!'

We scramble up a quite steep bit and then come to a rocky platform. Damon crouches to examine the ground. 'The Krypteian soldiers had built a fire to keep you warm. One of them was holding you; he would have been around seventeen and, I would bet, had never held a baby before!'

'What did Lysander do, when he was shown this place?'

'He demanded that my father be absolutely precise about the spot where the soldier was holding you. Then, he kneeled down and kissed the ground.'

'DOOMED TO LIVE BUT FOR A LITTLE SEASON'

My eyes blur at this vision of the small Lysander kissing the rocks where I was found. Damon says softly, 'He worshipped you, even then, Liddy.'

We look down at the foothills, where Peg and Hector are foraging, then out across the plains of Sparta. Damon says quietly, 'It's perfectly understandable that you're shocked and saddened at the death of someone you have served for so long. I'm sure that Lysander feels the same. But, don't you see, he had no chance of returning while Alexander was alive. And, now…'

I'm seeing Lysander smiling, becoming himself again, after telling me the awful news. Whispering, '*Trust me. I will find a way.*'

'Do you think…?'

'I don't think – I *know* he will return. And now, so must we, to get some food into you!'

*

Hope is a wonderful stimulant for the appetite. It meant that my poor mother no longer had to cast around for any delicacy that might tempt me to eat. Soon, I was back to my old ways of eating anything that was put in front of me, and then asking for more.

A few weeks after Damon and I went up the mountain, a young Krypteian officer comes to report to my father and Uncle Leon. Our two families gather to hear him, in the throne room where Alexander came to see us, all those years ago.

My mother wants to know if anyone has any idea what actually killed Alexander. He shakes his head. 'I'm afraid not, my lady. He had partaken of a large banquet the night before. And it is reported that, after the feasting, he met his young friend Medius of Larisa, who invited him to an afterparty, with more wine. The next day, he was very ill, and it was a decline that could not be halted.'

Uncle Leon asks, 'Is it known yet who his successor might be?'

The young man replies, 'During his last days, Alexander gave his ring to his vizier, Perdiccas, saying that he left his kingdom in the hands of "the strongest one". But his generals met the day after his death to discuss the new situation.'

My father comments, 'Because normally they, as representatives of the Macedonian nation in arms, would choose a new king.'

'And,' says my mother, 'the dead king has a brother, does he not?'

The young Krypteian replies awkwardly, 'I'm afraid, my lady, that Arridaeus is considered mentally unfit to rule.'

'Ah,' says Uncle Leon, 'so the matter now becomes highly complicated, and, I would guess, heated?'

'Indeed, sir. Perdiccas, who had, after all, been appointed by Alexander as his successor while he was on his deathbed, and was also the commander of the Companion Cavalry, said it was best to wait until Alexander's wife, Roxane, who was pregnant, had given birth. If the child were a son, it would be logical to choose him as the new king.'

My father laughs. 'Perdiccas is being too transparent! That would leave him in charge as regent until the boy had grown up.'

'It was a suggestion that Nearchus, the commander of the navy, objected to, sir. He said that Alexander already had a three-year-old son, Heracles, by his former concubine, Barsine.'

Uncle Leon comments, 'Easy to see through that proposal, too. Nearchus is married to a daughter of Barsine. As the future king's brother-in-law, he would suddenly become very influential.'

The young soldier acknowledges my uncle's point with a bow. 'The proposal was not even discussed, sir. Ptolemy, one of Alexander's close friends, spoke next. He objected to the idea that a son of Roxane or Barsine would be king of Macedon, because they were not full-blooded Macedonians. His proposal was that the most important decisions should be taken by those present, as some kind of collective leadership.'

Lady Danae smiles. 'I daresay that the military were not in favour of any kind of collective.'

'You are right, my lady. The commander of the phalanx, Meleager, objected, and sided with the king's brother, Arridaeus. He was supported by the foot soldiers, who hated Alexander's policy of bringing so many Persians into the army.'

Damon says, 'That must have created a very tense situation.'

'Indeed, sir. It seemed that Meleager's soldiers wanted to fight for Arridaeus against Perdiccas and his adherents.'

Damon nods. 'Effectively, a war between infantry and cavalry, an antagonism that has flared up before in Alexander's army.'

'It did get violent, sir. To the point where Meleager was killed. But eventually, the cooler heads on both sides came to a compromise. Perdiccas was to be regent for king Arridaeus and Roxane's son, if the baby turned out to be a boy.'

My mother says, 'Thank goodness sense eventually prevailed over violence.'

We heard later that Arridaeus became king under the name of Philip, and Roxane's baby was a son. We also heard that Alexander's second wife, Stateira, was murdered, which, we concluded, was Roxane's way of consolidating her son's position as heir. And I thought how humiliating it must have been for her to watch her husband marrying not one but two more wives at the ceremony in Susa. I imagine she was seeing red long before she found out what sex her child was.

*

Despite my mother's gratitude for good sense prevailing over violence, war had become inevitable. Athens had been preparing for war ever since Alexander's decree about the exiles was issued. As soon as they heard of Alexander's death, they revolted and were joined by many other Greek city-states (Sparta wisely kept out of it). Battles raged fiercely between Macedon and the members of the Corinthian League.

But some good came out of the many injustices that Alexander had done to his troops, especially the veterans who had been forced to settle in lands far away from their native Macedon. In the summer, Alexander's most successful general, Craterus (he who, you may recall, was just a bit too successful for Alexander's taste), arrived in Greece, leading back 11,500 veterans from Persia. He had also built Alexander's planned navy in Cilicia. Craterus used the fleet and the army to put an end to the war.

However, for one loser, there was a heavy price to pay. Athens should never have joined the war; they simply were not good enough at it without allies such as Sparta. Sadly, this time, we were in no position to help them. Sparta had spent years keeping Alexander off its back with our support for his campaigns. Athens ceased to be a democracy and became, instead of a free ally, a Macedonian subject, which we in Sparta thought was catastrophic. We will never embrace their system of governance, but it was tragic for them that they lost it.

At the same time, there was a revolt in the east from all those veterans who had been forced by Alexander to live in the new cities in the far eastern satrapies. Desperately homesick, they decided to fight their way back to Greece. On the way, without a general to lead them, they sustained terrible losses.

There was probably just one thing that was proved by the chaos that succeeded Alexander's death. He was the only force of nature capable of holding that massive empire together. When he went, it all went. Xenophon said it first, about empires and monarchy, when he wrote about the death of Cyrus the Great, the founder of the first Persian empire. He showed that empires in themselves lack stability and can be maintained only by a person of extraordinary prowess, such as Cyrus. Or Alexander.

At least Alexander got his dearest wish: both in Egypt, and elsewhere in the Greek cities, he received divine honours. His body, taken to Egypt by his friend Ptolemy, who was later to become pharaoh, was eventually placed in a golden coffin in Alexandria.

*

While all these theatres of war filled their stages with the clash of battle, my team and I threw ourselves into recruiting and training new Myrmidons. With the chaos around us, you never knew what new foe might suddenly threaten Sparta's freedom. On one exercise, we were running a rapid descent of the cavalry assault course, and everyone had done incredibly well, when Xanthippe comes up to me on her grey-dappled Heracles. She says, straight out, 'You're still waiting for Lysander, aren't you, boss?'

'For as long as it takes.'

'In that case, is it alright with you if I present my credentials to his brother? I've had this big thing for Damon ever since I was ten years old.'

And I thought I knew it all, when we boys and girls were small and naked and training together; I knew absolutely nothing at all. How dumb could I possibly be? We clasp hands, like we did at the Olympics, before that epic win. 'Go and make your happiness with Damon, sister. He is a lucky man!'

She told me later that Damon said he had been in love with her for as long as he could remember, but he was far too shy and admiring to dream of making an approach. So it was just as well that Xanthippe had no such inhibitions. I'm sure it was that same unhesitating boldness that made her an outstanding rider.

So now, preparations for many weddings between my Myrmidons and Lysander's cavalry went ahead. Both my father and my uncle deeply approve of weddings, because it means that more fighters can be bred in this warrior society. So they held three days of games to celebrate one mass wedding, where no fewer than thirty-two happy couples were tying the knot, headed by my best friend, Xanthippe, who was marrying her prince, Damon.

In the nights before the weddings, I start to dream again. I'm back in Alexander's tent, Lysander holding my head for me to drink. I didn't know that you could have a sense of smell in dreams, but as I gaze up at the sweetness of his countenance in the candlelight, I am breathing in the scent of his skin. Then, we're on the beach, where he's just told me, and all I can see is the heartbreak in his eyes, and that molten sun sinking into the sea. And now, we're passing each other on the podium steps, and it's the last time we can look at each other. And I see again that intense look of love in his eyes and feel the warmth of him.

The weddings went ahead in a perfectly glorious ceremony, which ended with a triumphant procession down the streets of Sparta, lined with cheering crowds, throwing flowers. I had thought that it could be extremely difficult to get through this, but it was made easier by my father and Uncle Leon insisting that I lead the procession. They reasoned that, after all, it was my initiative in volunteering to follow Alexander that kept him away from Sparta; this was as much a military triumph as a wedding celebration. I thought it was clever of them, because they knew I couldn't refuse. And after all, no one in those cheering crowds knew about Lysander and me. And, like me, all the brides and grooms were in their Spartan crimson, as all were in the army.

*

It was on the night of the weddings that a comet was first seen in the night sky. I don't mean a shooting star, gone in a flash. This comet was huge and bright, with a long tail, and it was there every night. Now, Spartans are not as obsessed as Alexander was in looking for divine meaning in everything, from what gate you use to enter Babylon to the weather. But this comet was an incredibly striking sight: beautiful, with its sparkling, golden tail streaming out behind it and lighting up the night sky with its brilliance. It remained with us for many months; on clear nights, crowds would gather to view it in awed silence.

I found the comet strangely compelling; often, I would saddle up Pegasus and ride to the foothills of Mount Taygetos to gaze up at the heavenly messenger. Seeing me now so much alone, with Damon and most of my girlfriends happily married, my father started to accompany me on these night-time excursions; it was very comforting to have him riding at my side.

One night, our horses are standing motionless as we gaze at the sky when my father touches my arm and points to a ledge twenty feet above us. Standing as still as a statue, his thick mane crowned by the silver light of the moon, is a huge wolf, looking down at us. But he isn't tensed to spring. His head is slightly on one side, as though he's thinking. The horses must surely have his scent, but weirdly, they are calm. So much so that, as the wolf seems to just melt from our sight, I wonder if we've seen a ghost.

During the ride back, my father tells me how he and my mother saw a wolf like that just before they encountered the Krypteia, led by Uncle Leon. When we get back and are settling the horses, the moon has disappeared from sight. But that magnificent comet blazes in the heavens for the rest of the night.

*

Once all the wedding excitement was over, and things got back to normal, I was asked by Uncle Leon to prepare a full account of Alexander's campaigns, to see how Sparta might be able to learn from the strategies and tactics employed. This brings me straight up against a monster of a problem: the whole reason why Alexander went to war. So I go in search of my uncle, as he was the one who briefed me on Alexander in the first place. He suggests a ride, so I pick Hector, Lysander's handsome bay, who has settled in well at Danae's stables; Uncle Leon accompanies me on his old friend, Arion. A warm breeze is blowing gently from an azure sky as we head out towards Mount Taygetos. Walking the horses by a stream, I feel a huge gratitude to be far away from those arid deserts that, time and time again, nearly killed us. As I collect my thoughts,

Uncle Leon says with a gentle smile, 'Out with it, Liddy. What is annoying you?'

'I have a problem with Alexander's motivation, Uncle. I mean, Lysander and I knew exactly why we were going to war – it was to protect Sparta! And you and my father knew exactly why you were attacking the Persian army.'

He nods. 'Defensive actions, in both cases.'

'He said, when he came to see us, that it was revenge he was seeking. He wanted to punish the Persians for invasions that had happened way back in the past. And yet the most recent invasion was completely defeated. As were the previous two.'

Uncle Leon says thoughtfully, 'Alexander was taught for four years by Aristotle, but I'm not sure whether that shaped his philosophy.'

'And Aristotle says, "We make war that we may live in peace." I'm not sure that Alexander was ever interested in living in peace, Uncle.'

'Aristotle also said, "It is not enough to win a war; it is more important to organise the peace." It would seem that Alexander's peace-making efforts may have been rather rushed.'

'He was always in a hurry. He couldn't wait to get on with the next battle. Even just before he died, he was planning to invade Arabia, Carthage, Sicily, and Italy!'

'Who had offered him no aggression. I think you will have to settle for "war for war's sake" with Alexander, Liddy. And now, we need to turn for home, as a visitor is coming for an audience this afternoon. You could be very interested in what he has to say.'

'DOOMED TO LIVE BUT FOR A LITTLE SEASON'

'Don't keep me in suspense, Uncle!'
'He brings news from Susa.'

*

As Uncle Leon and I enter the throne room, we find my father already there. He motions me to a seat between the two kings, which takes me aback; I had not thought that my military exploits would earn me this kind of honour.

The young Krypteian officer enters and bows, waiting to be questioned. My father leads: 'We gather that your news concerns the mass weddings that took place in Susa? Weddings which were the choice of neither party, in each case?'

The young officer bows again. 'Yes, sir.'

'And in these ceremonies, senior commanding officers of the Macedonian army were – in effect – ordered to take Persian princesses as wives?'

'Yes, sir.'

'Can you give us some examples?'

'General Craterus was ordered to marry Amastris, a niece of Darius. General Perdiccas married a daughter of Atropates. Ptolemy and Eumenes were to marry two daughters of Artabazus, Artacama, and Artonis. While Nearchus, the head of the navy, was given the daughter of Barsine. Seleucus took the daughter of the last leader of the Persian resistance, Spitamenes: a woman named Apame. And cavalry commander Prince Lysander married a princess named Calliope, sir.'

'Can you tell us what happened after the death of Alexander?'

'It became clear that most of the Greek commanders wished to divorce, having had these weddings thrust upon them, sir.'

'Is it known what their wives thought about this?'

'Many of them had already been promised to Persian princes. They were deeply unhappy at the forced weddings.'

Uncle Leon asks, 'Did these senior officers have to ask permission to divorce?'

'Their view was that, with Alexander dead, there was no one to ask permission from, sir.'

My father mutters, 'And while Alexander was alive, he would certainly not have granted it!'

'So,' continues Uncle Leon, 'have all these senior officers divorced their Persian wives?'

I hold my breath.

'There was only one officer who did not divorce his wife, sir.'

This is almost too much.

'And this officer is…?'

'Seleucus, sir, does not wish to divorce the princess Apame; she is of the same mind.'

My father asks, 'Have all these divorces been finalised?'

'I believe so, sir.'

'And is it known what has become of Prince Lysander?'

The young Krypteian officer hesitates, and I can hardly breathe. 'Regrettably, sir, our intelligence cannot trace him. After the wedding ceremonies, he was unable to maintain contact with us.'

*

'DOOMED TO LIVE BUT FOR A LITTLE SEASON'

After the interview is done, I say to my father, 'It would have taken this Krypteian officer at least three weeks to get here from Susa, yes?'

He nods. 'Probably more. They travel light, but there are many hazards, as you know well, Liddy.' He looks at me closely. 'You have a plan, don't you?'

'I know he is coming, Father. Can I borrow your sword again?' I had given my father his beautiful, deadly sword back soon after I returned home.

'You are going out onto the plains to meet him, aren't you?'

'Can you remember why you and my mother went up Mount Taygetos that night, after you received that terrible news about my namesake?'

Tears are in his eyes. 'It was all we had. All our young lives, we had herded sheep and roamed the mountain. We fell back on all we had.'

'This is all I have, Father. In all the life I have known with Lysander, our memories are mostly about sitting together in between battles and talking around a campfire.'

'Of course, you must go and wait for him.' He helps me to get my kit together. Including a good stock of arrows for hunting and his fearsome wolf sword. And I ride off on Peg, into the night.

I choose a place to camp which is close to the road into Sparta but on high enough ground to give me a good view of someone approaching from the mountains. I find I like being alone on the plains. During the day, I have enough supplies of food that I brought with me; no need to hunt, yet. And there is a river nearby, where Peg finds plenty of forage as well as water.

The first two nights are overcast, with no sign of the comet. On the third night of my vigil, the sky blazes with the light of the celestial visitor; and it continues for every night afterwards. During the day, travellers sometimes pass by, coming and going from Sparta. I am camped where I can see them, but they can't see me or my horse.

It's on the fourth night that I look down the road to the mountains and see the comet's light glinting on the helmet of a mounted warrior. His horse, pale in the glow of the comet, is walking gently, at a relaxed pace. When you've travelled thousands of miles to come home, you don't want to arrive completely worn out. My father told me how, when he had to ride Arion the Arabian from Babylon, to warn Athens and Sparta of the impending Persian invasion, he never asked more of his horse than the animal itself wanted to give; he said, no news on earth is worth the death of the messenger.

I stoke the flames of the fire until it becomes a beacon. But I'm sure he already knows. Nothing is going to prevent him from finding me. Now, as the rider comes closer, I can see that he is definitely in Spartan armour; the gleam of bronze in the light of that heavenly trail is unmistakeable. He is riding a white Arabian.

He arrives at my camp and slides off his mount; I take his mare to the river for water and food. I return to him, as he stands in the firelight, calmly waiting for me. I cannot see the eyes behind the mask of the helmet. But I know whose they are. I unbuckle his sword belt and lie his sword next to mine. I remove his breastplate and lie it on the ground, where it reflects the flames of the fire. Finally, I lift the helmet from Lysander's head, and the pale blond hair falls around his shoulders. I place the helmet on the ground, next to the breastplate. And stand, to see his blue eyes looking at me, like they did the very first time that I simply had to kiss him. Moving closer to him, I can feel the warmth of his body, like I fleetingly did in our last encounter, on the steps to the podium at Susa. Only this time, there will be nothing fleeting about anything that we do.

Glancing up at the torch in the sky and then turning to me, he says quietly, 'Are we to be eloquent witnesses again, do you think, my lady?'

The Laconian answer, of course, would be a quick 'no'. But now is not the time for brevity; this is love, not war. In reply, therefore, I embark on my one and only attempt at poetry; I've probably read it somewhere, as it's not the way I would ever normally speak. 'Eloquence, my lord, is a poor pastime for our lips.'

And so, we silence each other. And I don't give a fig if the conflagration above is divine or simply a gift of nature. The squabbling gods can do whatever they please, while I lie at last in my lover's arms, on the plains of Sparta.

This book is printed on paper from sustainable sources managed under the Forest Stewardship Council (FSC) scheme.

It has been printed in the UK to reduce transportation miles and their impact upon the environment.

For every new title that The Book Guild publishes, we plant a tree to offset CO_2, partnering with the More Trees scheme.

For more about how The Book Guild offsets its environmental impact, see www.bookguild.co.uk